ALLIGATOR
Skin

AudraKate Gonzalez

ISBN: 9798395187864

Stay spooky!

This book is dedicated to my siblings.

I'd fight off any monster for you dweebs.

THIS IS NOIR
Book 2: Louisiana

THIS IS NOIR:

Noir exists everywhere, and in every Noir weird stuff is always happening. Ghosts, monsters, ghouls, and more reside there. The destination is set, so travel across the states for chills, thrills, and things that go bump in the night.

Beware of false teachers who come disguised as harmless sheep, but are wolves and will tear you apart.

Matthew 7:15 TLB

PROLOGUE

Beep...Beep...Beep...

My arm twitches at the noise, my eyelids feeling too heavy to open. Groaning, I roll over, away from the annoying sound. The blanket shielding my body from the cool air feels scratchy against my skin. Kicking off the itch inducing material, I try to force myself back into a deep sleep.

Beep...Beep...Beep

It must be my alarm clock attempting to wake me, but the longer it rings in my ears, I realize it doesn't sound like an alarm clock at all. Even though it pains me to do so, I pry my eyes open.

The light around me is unbearably bright. I must have been asleep most of the day. As my vision begins to focus, the white, sterile walls come into view. The smell of disinfectant invades my nostrils. My heart jumps to my throat, and I lay there frozen.

This isn't my room.

I leap up from the bed to run, but my legs are like jello, pulling me down to the ground. A huge monitor crashes next to me and tugs on tubes and wires attached to me, stinging my arm.

The monitors go wild, switching from the annoying *beep* to blaring bells and whistles. Footsteps pound across the linoleum floor outside the door to the room. I feel like I'm going to be sick, which is bad, but I guess it's a good thing I'm already in a hospital. I try to push myself up from the ground, but my body doesn't have the strength to do so, and I sink back onto the floor. The paper-thin night gown makes me feel exposed and uncomfortable. I curl into a tight ball to cover myself.

A nurse clad in teal scrubs comes bursting through the door, her brown hair spilling from a ponytail. Her eyes grow wide when she sees me lying on the floor. Running over, she lifts me, and I slump over like a limp noodle in her arms. I haven't done anything, but I'm already exhausted from the shock of being in an unknown place.

When the nurse puts me back onto the bed, I see that her badge says her name is Misty. I like that name.

Wait...what's my name? I can't remember my own name

and that sends a jolt of fear through me.

I don't know how I got here. I don't know why I'm here. And I don't remember my name!

Sweat breaks out across my body. I feel incredibly hot and cold all at the same time. A vice grips my lungs, seizing my breath. My throat feels swollen, like an egg is trapped in my gullet, causing me to hyperventilate. Shadows start to creep into my vision, the room becoming a tunnel as the panic attack takes over my body.

Misty swipes a hand across my forehead, brushing her fingers through my hair to calm me.

"Shhhh, you're going to be okay," she gives me a small smile. "Doctor!" Misty shouts into the hallway, "she's awake!"

Awake? How long have I been...asleep?

CHAPTER ONE

Beep...Beep...Beep.

My hand slams down on the alarm shouting at me from my nightstand. I wish today wasn't happening. I wish I could go back to sleep, and everything could go back to the way it was before I ended up in a coma.

Mom pokes her head through the door. "Hey Jenny, time to get up. Don't want to miss the first day of school!"

Except, I do want to miss the first day of school. I don't want to go and deal with everybody staring at me. Do you know what it's like to miss four whole years of your life? Well, let me tell you. One minute, you're enjoying your life as an eleven-year-old, carefree child, then you get attacked by some animal, and the next thing you know, you're fifteen and you're expected to start high school.

The butterflies fluttering around in my stomach turn to a rumble and it starts to make me feel like I'm either going to barf all over or crap my pants. Both are terrible possibilities.

"I mean it Jensen, it's time to get up," Mom says as she passes by the door.

Annoyed, I groan and force myself out of my bed, leaving the comfort of its warmth. For someone who spent four years in a deep sleep, you'd think I'd never want to oversleep again, but I love sleep more than anything. I feel safe when I'm asleep, like nothing in the world can touch me in my dreams. If I were Sleeping Beauty, I'd probably punch any prince trying to wake me up in the face.

Flicking my bathroom light on, I'm greeted by my terrifying bedhead in the mirror. When I was in the hospital, my head was shaved for various medical procedures. It's been nine months since I was released, and in those nine months my hair has grown into a decent looking pixie cut and that is barely able to hide my scars.

With my coppery hair, I'd probably hate the pixie style, if it wasn't for Molly Ringwald. *Pretty in Pink* came out six months ago, and Molly Ringwald makes short, ginger hair look so cool. If only Mom would let me get a perm.

Even though there are some days that I hate my hair, I've

been pretty grateful to have an easy hairstyle. My strength hasn't come all the way back yet, so my arms can't handle brushing or styling my hair for very long. The first month I was home, I had to use a walker around the house. It's taken a lot of therapy and hard work to get me to where I'm at today.

After fixing my mess of hair into a tamer style, it's time to pick out my outfit, but I have no idea what to wear. I've spent the last nine months studying every Seventeen magazine to see what outfits are popular for the nineteen-eighty-six season. Leather, crop tops, shoulder pads, and high-waisted jeans are all the rage, but it's been a challenge trying to get Mom talked into any of the latest trends.

The problem with her is that she's having a hard time accepting the fact that I'm a teenager now. Heck, I have a hard time with it too. Not only did I miss four years of my life, but she also missed four years of her daughter growing up like a normal girl. In her mind, I'm still eleven. But the reality is that I'm not eleven anymore, so I need to fit in.

I've spent most of my time at home between recovering and catching up on school via homeschooling. I feel confident about being a sophomore, but I don't feel confident about being the new kid at school. I'm not really a new kid. I've been going to Noir schools since preschool. Odds are that most of the kids in high school are kids I knew growing up, but I have no idea who they are now. They might know me, but any memories I had before the accident have been completely erased from my mind.

Four years ago, I was walking home from a night of trick-or-treating with friends when, according to the doctors, an animal attacked me. I was found on the side of the road, bleeding. The good Samaritan who had found me rushed me to the hospital. The doctors performed immediate surgery to close any wounds and stop the bleeding.

They placed me in a medically induced coma, but when they tried to wake me after I became stable, I stayed in a state of unconsciousness. Nobody could figure out why. It took four years for me to finally wake up on my own. No one has ever found the animal that did it, but there is speculation that either a coyote or gator caused the injuries. Thankfully, the only permanent injuries I have are the ones I'm able to cover with my hair.

I'm pretty nervous about people asking me questions about the accident. There isn't much I can tell them, and I don't want to be known as "coma girl." That would be tragic. I just want to be me. Jensen Swells of Noir, Louisiana. And I sincerely hope that people are cool with that. I'd hate to make friends solely based off the accident.

After looking over my outfit options, I settle on a pastel pink shirt paired with a white button-down, high waisted jean, and my brand-new Nike's. The only jewelry I wear is the necklace my dad picked up at an old antique shop for me when I was a baby. He'd told me all about how I was his sunshine and that the necklace was a reminder of that.

The gold pendant has an archaic symbol that resembles a sun; a circle with beams fanning out in every direction. I was wearing it the day of the accident. The original leather strap my dad said had come with it had snapped during the attack. He'd fixed it with a brand new, thin, gold chain and gave it to me the day I came home from the hospital.

It doesn't really match my outfit, so I tuck it under my shirt.

I do a once over in my full-length mirror. Maybe not the most striking ensemble, but at least I won't stand out in the crowd.

I make my way to the stairs, backpack slung over my shoulder, and my sister, Linda, races past me and leaps off the last step.

Linda, who I apparently used to call 'Linny,' is seven now. She was just a toddler when I went into the hospital. She remembers as much about me as I do about her, which makes our relationship a little awkward. Mom and Dad used to take her to the hospital with them to visit me, but she never really understood everything. She's spent most of her life feeling like an only child, and then I came back into the picture. We're both still adjusting to living in the same household.

Breakfast is spread out across the kitchen table in a "choose your own" fashion. Bananas, pancakes, eggs, bacon, and orange juice are the options for the morning. Mom really went all out for the first day of school. Usually, breakfast consists of two options: cereal or oatmeal. Even with all the amazing foods littering the table, my stomach only wants one thing: blueberry muffins.

Blueberry muffins are the only thing I absolutely crave. I think about them all the time, and I know that we still have one left in the pantry, resting in a tiny Tupperware container.

Opening the pantry door, I look to where I last saw the muffin. Not there. My eyes scan the shelves as my hands rummage through them. No muffin.

"Hey Mom, do you know what happened to the blueberry muffin--" my words slowly trail off as I pull away from the pantry to see Linda, stuffing her face with *my* muffin.

"Are you serious right now?" I say, annoyed by the crumbs coating Linda's lips. Linda just shrugs her shoulders, her long blonde hair bouncing behind her. "That was *my* muffin. I was saving it specifically for today."

"You snooze, you lose." Linda responds, wiping the muffin crumbs off her face with her sleeve. That little punk. "Besides,

Mom made plenty of breakfast this morning."

"I'm aware, but you know that blueberry muffins are my favorite." I can barely control the anger in my voice.

"I know that? How could I possibly know that blueberry muffins are your favorite?" Linda retorts.

"Hm, because I've been eating them every morning since I came home!" I shout, and since I just can't help myself, I knock the rest of the muffin out of her hands and onto the floor. If I can't have it, then nobody will. A childish thought, I know, but one I can't help.

"JENSEN!" Linda wails and it, of course, gets Mom's attention. Mom marches into the kitchen sporting her workout wardrobe. She's wearing a blue and yellow striped leotard over blue tights. Yellow leg warmers cover the bottom half of her tights, and her tennis shoes peak out from beneath them. Her golden hair is teased into a yellow scrunchie. I can smell her Aqua Net hairspray from across the room. She's probably planning on sweating a bunch today during her aerobics class. Mom loves aerobics, but she hasn't been able to go to classes as much with Linda and I both at home. Now that school is starting, Mom will be able to frequent the gym more.

"Jen, really? You're really going to start with her on the first day of school?" Mom wraps Linda up in a hug while Linda cries her crocodile tears. I can't believe Mom is falling for any of this. Linda loves to cause all kinds of problems now that I'm back, and I end up being the one to always get in trouble for it because I'm "the oldest." It's funny how Mom wants to treat me like a child until she wants me to act my age around Linda. I wish I could get some sympathy from time to time. I guess giving me the punishments is our parents' way of making me feel like a normal teenager.

"Sorry, Linda," I say in my sincerest voice. Linda sniffs in response. The faker.

"There. Now hurry up and get your stuff together. We need to leave in five minutes." Mom walks away. With Mom out of sight, I stick my tongue out at Linda and she storms out of the kitchen. She won't tell on me for that, but she will use it to her advantage in the future.

The door of the refrigerator squeaks open as I scan its shelves for milk. The carton is hiding behind days of leftovers and items for making school lunches. My family isn't huge on drinking milk, and I know that I'm probably the only one regularly drinking it. I hope it isn't expired. Pulling down a glass from the cabinet filled with cups, the picture on the carton catches my attention. Another kid missing.

Penelope Fink. Date missing: 08/14/86. From: Noir, Louisiana. DOB: 04/26/70. White female, green eyes, height is 4'8, weight is 89 pounds, hair color is brown.

That's the third kid I've seen on one of these milk cartons in the past three months, and this one is around my age. I wonder if I knew her at some point in my life. I guess it's not safe for a kid to go anywhere anymore.

"Hey, sport!" Dad comes in and claps a hand on my back, bending over to kiss my forehead. He's ready for the workday with his button-up shirt, and navy-blue dress pants, that are pressed to perfection thanks to my mom. My dad has strawberry blonde hair that's not as red as mine. I definitely get most of my looks from him. "Ready for your first day back at school?"
I kiss him on the cheek. "As ready as I'll ever be."

"We'll celebrate your first week back this weekend. Just me and you. How's that sound?"

"Fishing?!" I ask, barely able to contain my excitement.

"Fishing." He gives me a big grin.

"Jen, it's time to go." Mom comes into the kitchen and gives Dad a hug, grabbing her purse and keys from the counter in the process. I follow Mom outside. Linda is already in the car. She's taken over the front seat, which should be mine, but I'm not about to fight her over it. Mom already took her side once this morning, and it'd be sure to happen a second time.

The sun is shining, and the air is sticky. Even though we're nearing the end of August, Noir will still reach somewhere around ninety degrees today. Fingers crossed that the school has air conditioning.

Getting in the car, my stomach tightens. I shouldn't be as nervous as I am. I've been preparing for this day for a while with test preps, meet and greets, the whole shebang. None of that seems to matter today. It's the real deal. Before, it was just prepping, and now it's happening. I've survived a lot, but for some reason I get the feeling that high school may just eat me alive.

BREAKFAST BLUEBERRY MUFFINS

What you'll need:

1 batch of Blueberry compote

½ cup (one stick) of unsalted butter, melted and cooled

2 eggs, room temperature

2/3 cup of whole milk, room temperature

1 tsp vanilla extract

1 Cup of brown sugar

2 cups of flour

¼ tsp salt

2 tsp baking powder

Directions:

Preheat oven to 350 degrees. Whisk together flour, salt, and baking powder and set aside. In a separate bowl, whisk together eggs, milk, melted butter, and vanilla. Add brown sugar and mix. Once combined, slowly add in the dry ingredients.

Batter will be thick.

Line a muffin tin with liners and fill each one 1/3 of the way with the muffin batter. Add 1 tbsp. of compote to each one and top with remaining batter. Top muffins with remaining compote (about 1 tsp. per muffin) and swirl with a toothpick.

Bake for 18-20 minutes or until tops are golden and inserted toothpick comes out clean.

Fruit Compote:

What you'll need:

2 C frozen fruit

¼ sugar

1-2 tbs water

Directions:

Add all ingredients to a saucepan and cook over medium heat, stirring occasionally, until sugar dissolves and fruit starts to soften. Turn heat to low and continue to cook, stirring frequently, until mixture starts to thicken. Remove from heat, cover and let cool.

CHAPTER TWO

The school building looks a lot different when it's filled with a bunch of students. When I visited a few weeks ago, it was only my parents, a few teachers, and the principal. But today there's so many students I feel like I may just drown. Nothing could have prepared me for this. Not even *Pretty in Pink*. Darn you, Molly Ringwald.

The grating sound of shoes squeaking against the linoleum floors echoes throughout the hallways. Lockers slam shut. Voices chatter all around. A pretty girl with gorgeous dark skin laughs along with the circle of friends that surrounds her. All the noises are enough to overstimulate my senses, throwing my body into overdrive.

My skin is prickling, and I feel myself wanting to shift into flight mode. I'd love nothing more than to turn around and run out the front doors. But I can't do that. I won't let myself do that. I'm already going to be "the new kid." I don't want to be "the new kid" *and* "the kid who ran out of the building on the first day."

Sucking in a deep breath, I make my way to my locker. Locker number thirteen. Lucky me. I'm not too keen on having that number, but the principal thought it best that my locker be near the entrance. My locker also happens to be next to the boy's bathroom. Gross.

The green hue of the lockers matches the floor and reminds me of vomit. My stomach churns at the thought. As if I didn't already feel sick, now I have to see these puke green lockers all day. I force a swallow.

No barfing today.

Not going to happen.

Spinning my lock from left to right, right to left, I put in the code to unlock it. My combination is the date I woke up. I figured it'd be easy to remember. The lock clicks open, but when I pull on the tiny handle of the locker it doesn't budge. I pull again with a sharp jerk. It still will not open.

"These lockers are always getting stuck because of the humidity." The cutest guy I've ever seen stands next to me and I'm totally at a loss for words. He'd give Rob Lowe a run for his money. His hazel eyes and black hair are enough to make me swoon. "You just have to hit it like this," he taps the locker with his fist. "And then pull up and towards you." A muscle twitches in his arm as he demonstrates the motion. "It always does the trick," he says, and the locker door springs open.

My throat is completely dry. Running my tongue across my lips, I try to moisten them, hoping I don't smudge my smokey rose lipstick in the process. It's the only makeup my mom would let me leave the house wearing. I swallow, unfortunately loud, to push past the dryness. "Wow. You're—uh —really good at that." I want to bang my head against the locker door for sounding so stupid.

"Well, I had to learn this on my own. I figure it's my job to let others in on the secret." He laughs and an adorable dimple appears in his left cheek, making me want to melt onto the floor. I have to mentally tell myself not to sigh out loud. "I'm Connor. I haven't seen you before. Are you new?" And there it is. The dreaded new kid questions begin.

I run a hand through my short hair, hoping he doesn't notice that it's shaking. "Yeah. I am... kind of." I wonder if I can possibly sound any more stupid.

"So, do you have a name? Or am I just supposed to call you new kid?" He smirks and there is that gosh darn dimple again.

"Oh, ew, please no," I laugh. "Jensen. My name is Jensen, but I'll respond to Jen." *Please call me Jen so I can hear what it sounds like when you say it,* I internally plead. I can't believe I'm hardcore crushing on the first human I've met today. Maybe I should have left the house more often these past nine months.

"Well, Jen," he says it and the sigh I've been holding in almost escapes me. "It's nice to meet you. I hope Noir High treats you well."

"So far, so good." I can't believe I just said that out loud. I silently ask God if He can just rewind this whole conversation for me. When I pictured myself one day meeting the guy of my dreams, I imagined I acted a lot cooler, like Molly Ringwald. But right now, I have a feeling that Molly Ringwald would be shaking her head.

I reach into my locker and pull out the books I'll need, the ones way too heavy to carry in my backpack. Connor can see me shift under the weight of the books in my hands, and he reaches out like he's going to take them from me. Then, just when my heart is fluttering at the thought that maybe he's about to carry my books, he pulls back as a girl walks over and places her arm across his shoulders. I recognize her as the beautiful girl I saw earlier laughing with her friends.

"Who's your new friend, ConCon?" Ew. ConCon? That's a terrible nickname. He should only ever go by Connor. To my relief, Connor rolls his eyes and shrugs her arm off. The girl looks a little put off by this, but not enough to deter her from looping her arm through his. She tosses her long, dark braids in my direction. She's spent a lot of time looking good for the first day of school. Her hair is done perfectly, and she picked out the perfect orange dress that accentuates her dark skin and matches her neon orange lipstick. I'm sure I look like a Troll doll next to her.

"I'm Jensen Swells." While I don't necessarily like this girl right off the bat, I still hold my hand out to her. She simply looks down at my outstretched hand, not in disgust, but more like she's deciding on if she likes me enough to touch my hand.

Recognition crosses her face, and her eyes flick up to me. Her eyelashes are accentuated by mascara. "Swells? You're the girl—"

I cut her off before she can finish because I really don't want Connor to know all about my hospital stay right now. I don't want pity, and I certainly don't want things to be awkward. "Yeah. I'm the new girl. And you are?"

She smirks. "Moira. Moira James." The bell chimes overhead, piercing my ears and making me jump. Moira pecks Connor on the cheek, he grimaces and steps away from her. "I'll see you two later then! Jensen, I'll have to show you around."

"Yeah, that'd be...great," I say as Moira takes off in the direction of her class, her black pumps clicking across the floor as she goes.

"Don't pay attention to Moira. She means well. She just

likes to show newbies that she's Queen B," Connor shrugs his shoulders, and I cringe at his use of the word "newbies." I don't think he notices my reaction. "So, what's your first class?"

I shift my books in my arms to pull out my schedule from the pocket of my jeans. "Looks like English with Mrs. Bern."

"Well then, right this way milady." Connor takes my books and ushers me down a long hallway past my locker. I blush at him carrying my books. From everything I've seen and read, when someone likes you, they tend to carry your books. I hope this is a good sign.

"This is it. English, room thirty-seven." Connor hands my books back. "I'll see ya around, Jen."

I smile as he brushes past me. He smells like melon and mint. I think that may be my new favorite scent.

Opening the door to room thirty-seven, I'm greeted by a stout woman with glasses sitting on the end of her nose, and her gray hair tied up into a tight bun. The room has plenty of natural light that fills the space. Famous quotes from various authors are plastered up on the walls.

"Forever is composed of nows. – Emily Dickinson."

"To be or not to be. —William Shakespeare."

Very…inspirational.

A chalkboard at the front of the classroom says "Welcome" in white chalk.

"Nice of you to join us," the woman grunts.

"Sorry, I'm Jensen Swells. I was looking for the classroom and—"

"Ah, yes. Miss Swells. Well, go find an empty seat. Class, say hello to our newest student, Jensen Swells."

A sea of staring students track me as I make my way to the only empty desk in the room. I shrink down as heads slowly turn in my direction. Most of them probably recognize my name. It was in the papers and on the local news for a while. I'm a medical marvel. Those who don't recognize my name are just staring because I'm the "newbie." My cheeks feel like they're burning. I wish they would just hurry up and turn around.

"Alright, now if I can have everyone's attention." The heads turn back to Mrs. Bern. Thank God. "There we go. Now let's get started."

CHAPTER THREE

Lunch comes sooner than I thought it would, and I'm relieved to have the break. Food doesn't sound super appealing right now, but I'm ready for the introductions to stop. I've heard "this is Jensen Swells" so many times today that I'm beginning to be sick of my own name.

The cafeteria is full of students, and while I could feel overwhelmed about it, it's more comforting than the intimate classroom settings. At least here I can get lost in the crowd. Everybody is too busy meeting up with friends they haven't seen in a while. Conversations about classes they hate, teachers they like, and what they did over the summer drift around me.

I assumed that I would be able to pick out the specific groups. Jocks. Popular. Goth. Preppy. Nerds. But it's nothing like the movies. Everyone looks the same to me. Just normal teenagers. Maybe this means I'll fit in easier. I can always hope.

Grabbing a blue plastic tray, I get in line for the food. My mom had asked me if I wanted my lunch packed last night, but I told her no. While I love my mom's peanut butter sandwiches, I've lived on her food for a while. It's time to venture out and try new things. But after seeing the cafeteria food, I think I'm going to regret this decision. Sloppy joes, peas, fruit, and french fries are the lineup for today. I'm not a vegetarian, but sloppy joes aren't exactly the most appetizing thing on the planet.

"How were your morning classes?" Moira squeezes in next to me, cutting off the person in line behind me, but they don't seem to mind. While there doesn't appear to be any defined cliques, Connor was right when he said that Moira is Queen B. I think the students here are okay with her walking all over them. Everyone needs a leader, I guess.

"They were pretty good," I say, placing a carton of milk onto my tray. Moira's tray is practically empty. She opts for only fruit and peas. No wonder she looks so good in that dress. Then again, maybe she knows something about the school's sloppy joes that I don't. My stomach grumbles in response.

"You can come sit with me at my table." Moira moves in front of me. Great. A seat at the Queen's table. I should feel honored, but I feel skeptical instead. There's a group of girls, and a couple guys sitting at Moira's table. I thought lunch would give me some quiet time to reflect on how my day has been going so far. I thought it would give me a break with all the introductions. But with Moira, that's not going to be the case. "Guys, this is Jensen Swells." That's it. I'm changing my name. "The new girl." Moira isn't a snob when she says it, but I still can't get a read on if she's trying to be friends with me or not. "Jensen, this is CeCe, Valerie, Mabel, Mark, and Greg."

I slowly set my tray down next to Moira's. "It's—uh—nice to meet you all."

"Oh, you're in my math class! It's nice to officially meet you." The girl named Valerie flips her blue-black hair and smiles at me.

"I bet all the stares have been annoying. I remember what it's like to be the newbie." Mark looks at me, then proceeds to take a giant bite out of his sloppy joe. At least he doesn't seem to think it's gross. Although, Mark is a broad guy, and even from his seated position, I can tell he's tall. He probably *needs* to eat the sloppy joe, no matter what it tastes like.

I pick up my own sandwich and Moira places a hand on mine. "Don't." She looks from me to the sandwich in my hands. "That is what we call mystery meat. You'll learn that it's safer to pack your own lunch. Unless it's pizza day."

"You didn't pack a lunch." I point to her vegetable and fruit covered tray.

"Forgot to with all the excitement of today," Moira shrugs. Taking Moira's advice, I put my mystery meat lunch back on the tray and scoop up a spoonful of peas instead.

"So, did you guys hear the news?" Mabel moves a dark curl away from her face and straightens her glasses. Mabel has a natural cuteness that makes me a little jealous. She has pale skin like me, but her cheeks have the perfect rosy hue.

"Yeah. It's all anyone can talk about." Greg adjusts his red baseball cap. His hat has a sports team on it that I don't recognize. Then again, I haven't watched a lot of sports since I've been home. I wonder if he's what would be considered a jock.

"I just can't believe it was her. She was always so nice." CeCe's bright green eyes have a misty film over them. Valerie hands her a tissue from her purse. These girls carry purses. Not backpacks. I must look super lame with my burly, black bag.

"I'm sorry, but, what news is it that everyone is talking about?" I ask, feeling very out of the loop. Consequences of being the new girl, I guess.

"Penny Fink went missing. And a week before the first day of school. Talk about tragic." CeCe dabs at a tear that's escaped, trying not to smudge her blue eye shadow. Moira wraps an arm around CeCe and soothes her by running her other hand through CeCe's dirty blonde hair.

"Oh. I'm sorry. I saw her picture on a milk carton this

morning. Was she a close friend of yours?" sympathy laces my voice, and my question causes CeCe to burst. She rushes away from the table and out the cafeteria door, her blonde hair floating behind her. "I shouldn't have asked that. The word vomit is real today." I hope the rest of them don't shun me from the table for my complete stupidity.

"Don't worry about it. CeCe reacts that way about everyone who has gone missing. I think she's just really freaked out that one day it could be one of us. Or maybe even her," Valerie checks her manicure as she speaks. Maybe it's because of all the crap I've already been through, but going missing isn't a fear of mine. Never waking up again is, however, a major fear that I have. Don't get me wrong, I love sleep. I'm obsessed with getting plenty of it. But that doesn't mean I don't fight going to sleep at night out of fear that I might not be able to wake up.

"It's totally plausible that anyone of us could be next."

"Please shut up Mark," Mabel swats Mark's arm.

"No. It's true. She's the third one since June, and the eighth since the beginning of the year. And that's not including the ones who went missing last year or the year before that," Greg chimes in.

Mark gets up from his seat. "The Boogeyman is hunting teens, and you're next!" Mark grabs Mabel's sides and squeezes. Mabel squeals in response, almost falling off the bench.

Everyone else at the table laughs, including me. It's the first time in a while that I've genuinely belly laughed. I can't believe I was nervous about today. While I'm still a little skeptical about Moira and her intentions, I can see myself fitting in really well with this group.

The bell rings, signaling that lunch is over and it's time to get back to classes. Picking up my tray, I dump most of my lunch in the garbage and place the tray on top. My stomach gurgles at the sight of all my wasted food. I'll be scarfing down dinner tonight for sure.

Moira runway walks up to me, braids swinging behind her. "Hey, you should totally come with us tomorrow night. A bunch of students and the PTA are going around to pass out flyers for the missing students."

"I—"

"Connor will be there," Moira winks. She's screwing with my head. First, she's all hands-on deck about Connor. Now she's trying to dangle him in front of me like some kind of treat.

"Aren't you into Connor?" I ask, which is bold of me.

Moira chuckles. "Connor and I were a thing, for a minute. And I'd be lying if I said I didn't still wish we were. But sometimes the fascination is simply because someone becomes the shiny new toy."

"Connor's new here, too?"

"He moved here a few years ago. Sometime around eighth grade, I think. We clicked last school year, went to a few dances together but, as I'm sure Connor will probably tell you, we're better off as friends."

I raise an eyebrow.

"I'm serious." Moira bumps my arm with hers. "Look, I know I come off a little rough around the edges. And I know you'll hear about all those 'Queen B' rumors. But that's really not who I am." Her voice drops low. "Kind of like how I know you're not just 'coma girl.'"

Moira surprises me. That whole "don't judge a book by its cover" saying is evidently true. I had her pegged for the mean girl that would ruin my life. I figured it would only be a matter of time before she spread the news about me.

I don't know if God is simply smiling down on me, giving me a break from bad times, but this is not what I expected for the first day of school. Everything that I imagined could possibly go wrong has actually gone... right. Which means that the worst is yet to come. Sorry for being a Negative Nancy, but that's how these things go. Can't be too optimistic, at least not with my luck.

CHAPTER FOUR

The last class on my schedule is Mythology and Folklore with Mr. Chaney. I haven't had a single class with Connor all day, and I haven't seen him walking around the hallways either. We must just miss each other with our class schedules, which is a mega bummer. Although, my parents will probably be happy about that. Odds are, with Connor sharing my classes, I'd be one hundred percent distracted.

To my surprise, when I walk into Mythology, Connor is sitting at the back of the room. *Consider me distracted.* And as if this day can't get any better, there is an empty desk right next to him. I would scream right now if I knew nobody could hear me.

Making my way toward the empty seat, I smile brightly at Connor. He gives me a half-smile that makes me internally panic. A half-smile can't be good, right? Or maybe it is good? Is a half-smile like a flirty thing?

Wait, did Seventeen ever say anything about guys that give you a half-smile? I scan my brain for that knowledge, but then another thought intercepts my focus. What if I have lipstick on my teeth and he's completely grossed out by it, resulting in a half-smile? I'm overthinking this way too much. It's a half-smile for goodness' sake! *Stay cool, Jen.*

"Hey." I slide into my seat, trying to remain calm. I hope he can't see me sweating. Oh my gosh. What if he *can* see me sweating? Lifting my arm, I run my fingers through my hair so I can nonchalantly check for pit stains. No stains. *Whew.*

"Hey, how's your day been?" Connor turns in his desk, giving me his full attention. His bright blue shirt mixed with the fluorescent lighting highlights the blue undertones of his pitch-black hair. I wonder if he even knows how amazing he looks. He should be gracing the pages of every teen magazine. They'd sell billions.

"It's been surprisingly good." Almost suspiciously good.

"I wish I could say the same. I can already tell that this year is going to kick my butt. Between football and homework, I'm not going to have much of a life." He runs his hands over his face in frustration.

"You play football?" I'm impressed.

"Yeah, but I can't say I love it," he shrugs. "My dad is super into it. I mostly do it for him, which I know probably isn't the right thing to do, but he's been through a lot, and he's been there for me." I'm curious as to what the situation is that makes Connor feel like he must play football for his dad, but I don't think it's something I should pry out of him.

"Wow. Sounds like your dad has one awesome son." My cheeks grow warm. Connor smiles at me, and it's the kind of smile that shows off his dimple. I wish I could make him smile all day, but we're interrupted by Mr. Chaney.

"Good afternoon, class. Welcome to Mythology and Folklore." He clears his throat. "I'm Mr. Chaney, but you can call me Mr. C." Mr. Chaney—I mean—Mr. C, appears to be younger than any of the other teachers. I would imagine he only finished college a few years ago. His brown hair is cropped short, and styled a little too much for my liking, and his beard could use a trim. With his polo untucked, and slightly wrinkled, my guess is he's probably single. "This is my first year teaching at Noir High. I moved here over the summer. Do we have any first-time students here?"

My hand hesitantly goes up. *Please don't make me say anything.*

"Awesome. Well, I hope we all have a good time learning together." He clearly knows what it's like to be a newbie. Mr. C starts the roll call, and while I'm focused on the names he's calling out, Connor pokes my arm. There's a balled-up note in his hand that I discreetly take.

This guy may turn out to be the coolest teacher all year.

I giggle and nod my head in response.

"Jensen Swells?" Mr. C looks up from his paper.

"Here," I say through my giggling. Honestly, it's not even like what Connor said was funny, but the fact that he passed me a note has me giggling like a complete fool. I need to pull myself together before he never speaks to me again.

"So, today I'd like to open with one of my favorite topics; cryptids." Mr. C looks at all of us with a gleam in his eyes. "Can anyone tell me what a cryptid is?" Absolute crickets follow as no one answers. Connor opens his mouth, like he wants to say something, but he stays silent. "That's alright, we're here to learn. Cryptids are animals believed to exist, but they are not accepted by modern science."

Oh great. This is going to be some kind of nerd class; I can already sense it. I'm about to roll my eyes in Connor's direction, but he leans forward in his desk, like he's really interested in what Mr. C is about to say. I guess this means I'm going to have to pay attention. I want Conner to see that we're into the same things, and if he's digging what Mr. C is saying, then so am I.

"Now, with that in mind, can anyone name a cryptid?" Mr. C lifts a piece of chalk to the board, ready to write down any answers given.

"Bigfoot!" someone shouts.

"Mothman!" another says. Mr. C frantically writes as names I've never heard of are shouted left and right. When Connor says, "The Jersey Devil," I decide I should join in too, even though I have no idea what I'm talking about.

"Werewolves?" I answer like I'm asking a question, obviously very unsure of myself. Connor looks at me and smiles which makes me feel better. But then Mr. C stops writing on the board, and I think that maybe I've said the wrong thing.

Mr. C turns toward the class. "Interesting answer, who was it—" he scans the room, and I slowly raise my hand. "Ah, Jensen. So, werewolves are interesting because they are shapeshifters. Cryptids are not typically related to humans, but werewolves are humans in animal form." Mr. C straightens his glasses. "So, based on this information, would you still classify them as a cryptid?"

Oh crap. Is he really asking me this question? I feel like my eyes are going to bug out of my head. Everyone is staring at me, waiting for me to give a response, but words are not coming to me. I can feel sweat starting to form on my brow, coming back with a vengeance. I keep my arms tightly at my sides, in case of stains. As all the gazes in the class shift toward me, I squirm in my seat.

"Well, considering that all cryptids have only anecdotal

evidence, no hard evidence for proof of existence, similar to a werewolf, I would say that werewolves are cryptids." Connor swoops in to answer, saving the day and making me want to kiss him. My cheeks warm at the thought. I hope no one notices the redness that's creeped up onto my face.

"Very good observation, Connor." Mr. C writes 'werewolves' on the board with all the other names. I mouth the words "thank you" to Connor and he gives me a slight head nod in return. Okay. So that wasn't a total trainwreck, but I should avoid answering any further questions until I can get a grasp on this whole cryptid thing. If it weren't for the fact that this is my only class with Connor, I'd drop it in a heartbeat.

"Most cryptids are derived from folklore that's been passed down through generations. In North American Native folklore, cryptids are seen as beings of strength and power, and they are held to great esteem. However, over the years cryptids have just been turned into stories of fiction, and many people believe they were invented as a way for others to cope with unnatural occurrences." Mr. C perches on the edge of his desk.

"Wait, so do you believe in cryptids?" I almost scoff, but I remember who I'm talking to. So much for keeping my mouth shut.

"I don't think hundreds and hundreds of years of sightings and stories is something to dismiss. Plus, many generations ago, cryptids were a huge part in Native culture, and I don't think that's anything to mock. But I do know that there will be many people who disagree with me on that," he shrugs his shoulders. "Which brings me to your assignment for this first semester." Oh great. Homework already. I can hardly wait. "You're going to take a cryptid, of your choice of course, and write an essay on whether or not you believe it exists."

"How are we supposed to believe something exists when there's only anecdotal evidence?" Connor asks.

"Then tell me why you don't believe it. Disprove the anecdotal evidence you find. Whatever you do, though, do it well. Make me either believe or disbelieve with you. If I'm not convinced, then that may mean a bad grade for you."

Great. I'm going to fail for sure.

"The library will be your best friend for this assignment. You guys will be presenting your chosen cryptid for class on Monday. Have a couple in mind because I don't want multiple students using the same cryptid. I highly encourage you to work on your essay with a buddy, if you want." I hope Connor wants a buddy on this one.

As the clock changes to three, everyone rushes from their seats and begin to pack up their bags right as the bell rings. They exit in stampede formation, like they're just dying to escape. I wait for the crowd to disperse before I gather my own things.

There's a tap on my shoulder, and I turn to face Connor.

"I think this class is going to be pretty fun. What do you think, partner?"

Partner? Is this his cute way of asking me to be his partner without asking me to be his partner? "Yeah, I mean I love learning about this kind of stuff." This kind of stuff? *Jen, you idiot.*

"What do you say we head to the library tomorrow night?"

Eek! Connor is asking me out! Okay, so he's not asking me out, but it kind of feels like that, so I'm just going to enjoy my internal freak out moment. And then I remember that we can't go to the library tomorrow night because we're both supposed to help pass out flyers for the missing students.

"We can't." The look of disappointment on Connor's face when I say that makes me feel good. "Not because I don't want to. I'd obviously love to go to the library with you, but we're supposed to pass out flyers tomorrow."

Connor's eyes light up. "Wait, you're going to that?"

I nod my head in reply.

"Oh sweet! I didn't realize you were going. That's why I asked about the library. But we can do the library on a different day! We do have a few more days before we have to give Mr. C our selections." Connor seems really excited, and it makes me happy. It's a good feeling to know that getting to hang out with me makes him this way.

"Well, I guess I'll see you around. I've gotta get out of here to—uh—pick up my little brother." Connor swings his backpack up onto his shoulder. Sweat beads across his forehead. It's not hot in the classroom. Maybe Connor's just nervous thinking about hanging out tomorrow.

"You—you drive?" As if he couldn't get more attractive.

"Don't sound too impressed. I drive my dad's old Pinto. A complete rust bucket."

"So, you're sixteen then?" I ask.

"Uh—yeah. I took driver's ed in the spring and turned sixteen over the summer. Getting my license was the only thing I wanted for my birthday, and for passing the test, my dad gifted me his old car."

"That's awesome!" I mean it when I say it, but there is a slight sadness that follows. I'm only fifteen right now but, even when I turn sixteen, I'm not sure if I'll be allowed to get my license. I think a doctor will have to sign off on letting me get one, and that may mean more tests to make sure I'm mentally and physically able to drive. The accident caused more problems than I ever thought it could, and I'm sure these problems will continue to come up in the future. I just need to tell myself not to dwell on it and enjoy life in the moment.

"Well, I guess I'll see you around tomorrow. It's been nice

meeting you, Jen." The twinkle in his beautiful, hazel eyes makes my heart beat a little faster.

"It's been nice meeting you too, Connor." I give him a slight wave as he walks away. I love school.

CHAPTER FIVE

I hate school.

It should be a crime to give students homework on the first day. Mythology and Folklore may sound like a fun class, but I think it's going to be the death of me. I wanted to learn about the Greek Gods, like Aphrodite or Athena. I didn't want to read page after page on some furry beast out of a *Dungeons and Dragons* game.

Even though I hate this assignment, I take advantage of the fact that no one is home, and the house is quiet, and I get started on my crafting ideas for my essay.

Connor had mentioned getting together at the library to pick our cryptid before Monday, but I want him to see I'm knowledgeable on the subject, so I need to do some research before.

The book given for the class, called *The Encyclopedia of Cryptids*, doesn't have any interesting topics that I want to cover. Bigfoot, The Loch Ness Monster, Mothman, and The Jersey Devil don't pique my interest, but I at least know a little bit more about each of them.

The Loch Ness Monster, or as many people refer to it, Nessie, has been around for centuries, so the stories say. Nessie has become a staple piece in Scottish folklore. It's the same for all of these creatures. They're all a part of some region's folklore, passed down through generations, and almost every State has once.

New Mexico has La Llrona; an evil looking woman who kidnaps children that look like her own. Alaska has the Tizheruk; a serpent-like creature that hunts in the cold waters. Minnesota has Wendigo, so on and so forth.

It has me wondering about Louisiana. Louisiana is well known for its dark magic, and voodoo practices, but what other monsters lurk around here that aren't talked about? Everyone knows about Marie Laveau, the voodoo queen of Louisiana, but she isn't a cryptid. What Louisiana myths have faded into the background? That's what I want my essay to be on.

With my decision made, and my knowledge of cryptids grown a little, I put the books away. Perfect timing, too, because the front door creaks open, and I hear Linda come bouncing through it, humming some annoying tune I'm sure she heard from the little kid playground. How can anyone be so energetic after a full day of school?

"Jen?" Mom calls up the stairs.

"Be right down!" I holler. Linda bursts into my room. "Didn't I tell you to knock before you come barging in here, creep?"

Linda narrows her eyes. "Call me creep one more time and I'll get Mom and Dad to get rid of your door for good."

"And how exactly would you manage to do that?" I cross my arms. She's pretty convincing, but I don't know if she's *that* convincing.

"Don't doubt me. I have my ways." She jumps onto my bed, making me want to scream. Linda really knows how to test my patience. I don't understand how I ever got along with her before. Maybe it was because she was a cute little toddler then. "So, how was your first day of school?" Is that sincerity I hear in her voice? I shake my head. There's no way.

I swat her with a pillow. She bellows like it really hurt her. I know it didn't. "School was fine. Now would you please leave? You're getting your annoying little germs all over my clean bed."

"I don't have annoying germs!"

"I beg to differ," I roll my eyes at her. Linda kicks off the bed and stomps out of the room. I'd like to be able to take this as a win, but I know she's only stomped off to tattle, and the conversation will be the same. Another lecture on how I'm the older sister and need to act like it. I can never catch a break. The upside is that Mom doesn't go easy on me just because I've been through the ringer. That probably doesn't sound like an upside to most, but to me it is.

Being held responsible for the arguments between Linda and I isn't always a bad thing. Sure, it drives me crazy most of the time, but it also means that Mom is recognizing that I *am* older. I'm hoping that it'll mean one day she'll treat me like I'm older in all areas of my life. Like maybe dating...

Mom is in the kitchen cutting potatoes for dinner. Dad should be home in the next hour or so, and we have dinner as a family as soon as he gets here every single evening. It's been my favorite part of the day for a while. It's the only time that Linda and I don't fight, because we're too busy laughing at Dad and the things he says. His dinner stories are always top notch. For example, for last night's story, he talked about one of his patients who had a booger in his nose.

My dad is a dentist, so when one of his patients came in and had a booger in his nose, he discreetly sucked it up with the saliva ejector when the patient's eyes were closed. The whole family was roaring in laughter. I don't think Mom loved the story, especially at the dinner table, but it didn't stop her from laughing along with the rest of us.

"Need some help?" I ask, picking up a carrot and the peeler.

"That'd be great." She smiles at me. I scan the room and don't see Linda anywhere. Leaning over the counter, I peek through the doorway into the living room. Linda had gotten distracted by a *Scooby Doo* episode, the one with the Creeper, an absolute classic if you ask me. Her distraction means she didn't get a chance to tell on me. Thank you, Scooby Dooby Doo.

"School was good today?" Mom raises an eyebrow at me.

"Yeah. It was really good," I sigh.

"Did you meet anyone new?" Mom knows that I hate the term "make any friends" because it sounds childish. She used to ask me if I made any friends after every physical therapy session and it would drive me crazy. I finally had to politely ask her to stop.

"I did! And they've invited me out tomorrow evening." I nervously chew on my lower lip. I'm not sure how she's going to react to me wanting to go out tomorrow. I can see the struggle in her dull grey eyes that look so much like my own. The only thing that my mom passed on to me. Linda is her carbon-copy, with her platinum blonde hair and small, wiry frame.

The thin line of her lips means she's weighing her next words. Does she let her teenage daughter go out so her daughter can feel more normal? Or does she say "no" because she doesn't think her daughter is ready?

"While I think that's great, Jen, I'm just not sure…"

"It's not like a real hangout, though. We're passing out flyers for the missing kids. The PTA will be there and everything." Her blonde eyebrows raise at hearing that. Maybe I should have led with the "PTA" thing.

"You'll be safe?" She purses her lips.

"Totally!" I should probably cool it on the excitement in case she's still planning on crushing my hopes.

"And you'll be home before dark?"

"You know me, Miss Afraid of the Dark," I joke. Mom sets down the potato she's cutting and stares at me. I guess we're being serious. "I promise I'll be home before dark, and if I'm not, you can ground me for life."

Mom resumes cutting the potato. "Alright, you can go."

I wait for the "but." There's an awkward moment of silence, and I begin to think she might not say anything else.

"But—" and there it is. "You stay with the group. Don't go wandering off, and absolutely no talking to anybody alone. There are too many strange people out there."

CHAPTER SIX

It's a crisp, late, August evening that teases an early Fall, but you know it's going to be scorching in the morning. The scent of rain is in the air, the humidity still lingering and, as darkness rolls in, I wonder exactly how long we will be able to hand out flyers before the clouds open on us.

I chose to wear my yellow rain boots and a light jacket, just in case. Now I'm wondering if I should have accepted my mom's ugly, floral umbrella. It's gigantic, and a little embarrassing to carry, so I politely declined her offer. Seeing all the other students walking around with their umbrellas makes me think I made a mistake. Oh well, too late now.

We all meet outside the front of the school. It's weird being out here when school isn't in session. The boring, brown building looks like a prison against the gloomy sky. The American Flag whips around in the wind that is starting to pick up.

Parents and teachers alike are passing out stacks of flyers to all the students. I awkwardly stand there, shivering in my jacket, looking for anybody I know. There is no sign of Moira or anyone else I recognize anywhere. Maybe Moira was lying about coming? It's possible that this is some kind of trick to make me look like a real dweeb. Although, I'm not sure how passing out flyers for missing kids would make me a dweeb. Besides, she brought it up again today at lunch and everyone at the table seemed eager to help in any way possible. Then again, it's possible something came up and they couldn't come.

I'm about to turn around and go home when Moira pops up behind me, causing me to practically jump out of my skin.

"Glad you could make it, Jensen." Moira beams at me, showing her insanely white, perfectly straight teeth. Welp. Guess you'll never catch me smiling next to her. I'm already super self-conscious about the gap between my two front teeth, but seeing her smile makes it even worse.

Moira is wearing a bright pink cardigan, and an acid wash denim skirt. She has a pink umbrella, that matches her cardigan perfectly, over her head. I don't know how she isn't cold, but at least she looks fashionable. Her braids are pulled back into a ponytail, and the only makeup she's chosen is a light sweep of mascara. I hope it's waterproof, for her sake.

"I'm glad my mom agreed to let me out of the house." Ugh. That sounds so lame.

"I can imagine with everything you've been through that your mom keeps a close eye on you." Moira is spot on about that. It makes me smirk to hear her say that, though. Moira gets me, and I appreciate it.

"It's gotten better. I think she realizes she can't keep me locked up forever. I'm not eleven anymore." I rub my arms. "Aren't you chilly?" I ask, trying to get the topic off myself.

Moira laughs. "Never let the weather ruin your outfit. Fashion over comfort. Always." Moira eyes me up and down. I'll admit, my outfit isn't runway ready in the least, but fashion over comfort doesn't sound too practical to me. While I do love her sense of style, I won't be taking clothing advice from Moira any time soon.

Mabel comes running across the front lawn, umbrella bouncing in her hands. Mark strolls up behind her, throwing his arm over her shoulder. Mabel looks at his arm in disgust and throws it off her. I hear Moira snicker at the two of them, and I join in with her.

Mr. C stops by and drops a stack of flyers in mine and Moira's hands. "Thanks for joining us, girls. It's nice to see students being so supportive." He wipes off his glasses that are starting to fog. "If you guys could take Canal Street to Ridge that'd be great. Take as many in your group as you want. The more the merrier!"

Mabel and Mark reach us as Mr. C walks away. Moira passes half of her stack to Mabel, and I do the same for Mark. He flips through the flyers with a sad look on his face. "I still can't believe that they're all missing. It feels so weird."

Mabel places a hand on his arm. Even though I've never met any of these kids, or at least don't remember any of them, I still feel the same wave of sadness. Mark was right yesterday; it could have been anyone of us. It could still be anyone of us. No one has been caught and, as far as I know, there aren't any leads.

The police have been trying to make the community feel better about the situation. The only thing they ever say is "we're working hard to find whoever is doing this." Which to me isn't too reassuring. They can work as hard as they want, but without any leads, or evidence for that matter, what can they really go off of?

"CeCe and Valerie want us to meet them at CeCe's dad's store," Mabel pulls her curls up into a bun while Mark holds her umbrella and flyers.

"CeCe's dad owns a store?" I ask.

"Oh, yeah. Her dad owns the appliance store on Main.

CeCe and Val both work there." Moira leads our group down the sidewalk.

"Shouldn't we wait for Connor and—" my words are cut off as Connor and Greg make their way toward us.

"Speak of the devil." Moira winks at me. Connor has his dark hair perfectly in place, and he's still wearing the white and green striped button-up I saw him wearing earlier in class. I didn't get the chance to talk to him after class today. He booked it out of there pretty fast, most likely to pick up his little brother from school. I think it's sweet that he's such a good big brother. If Mom ever asked me to pick Linda up from school, I'd throw a fit. Maybe I can learn a thing or two from Connor.

"I almost didn't want to come," Greg flexes his jaw.

"Then why did you?" Moira glares at him like he's ruining her mood.

"Because this guy dragged me along," he jabs a thumb in Connor's direction. "This whole thing is just too depressing. And this weather sucks."

"Well, I bet if Penny knew you were out here helping, she'd be super happy." Moira stomps off ahead of us.

There's clearly some kind of tension there. I want to ask about it, but I feel like it's not my place being the new person in the group and all. Turns out that Connor seems to want me to understand what's going on. He leans in closer to whisper.

"Penny had a thing for Greg last year. He never gave her the time of day, and now that she's missing, Moira's sour with him for the way he treated her. Not that Moira treated her a whole lot better. I think she's beating herself up about it too." He rubs his chin. "It's probably another reason she's been so nice to you."

I'm offended. "Why? Because she thinks I'm kidnapper bait?"

Connor laughs. "No. Not that at all. I just think she has a lot of regrets about the way she's treated people in the past. Moira's turning over a new leaf." That makes sense to me, and I'm glad that Moira's decided to change her ways. I'd hate to have started school during a time when Moira wasn't trying to be nice to everybody.

We walk up and down various streets to get to Main. It's weird how none of this looks familiar to me. I know how to get to school, and home. I know where my dad's dental office is, but aside from all of that I don't really know Noir. The town is cute. Swampy flatlands mostly, but also very cookie cutter in a lot of places. White picket fences are a staple piece in most yards. All the houses are average sizes and painted in various shades of white and beige. There is also an Old District in Noir and all the houses still have their French architecture. Our Dad takes us there occasionally. I've never cared for it, but my dad swears that when we go there this Winter to see all the Christmas decorations, I'll love it. I guess the Old District goes all out for the Holidays.

It's hard knowing I've lived here my whole life, but I have no recollection of the place. Did I know Noir before the accident? Was there a time when I would run all over the town, with no fear of getting lost or attacked by a wild animal? Will Noir ever feel safe for me again?

I find myself trying to stay in the middle of the group as we move. Every corner we pass gets a second glance from me. There are too many unknowns out here. Not only am I concerned about the animals that lurk around in the shadows, but now I have to be concerned about a kidnapper. It's all I can think about as we walk.

"So, do you?" Connor touches my arm, and I realize he's been trying to talk to me. The thoughts in my head and the sights around me have been so distracting that I haven't been paying attention to the conversation going on.

"I'm sorry. What was the question?" I can feel the heat rising to my cheeks.

"Oh, we were talking about roller skating. Greg and I just got some new skates and thought it would be fun to go sometime. So, do you like to skate?" Do I like to skate? I have no idea! I don't even know if I know how to skate. That wasn't something I concerned myself with once I got home from the hospital. I was so focused on catching up on the latest trends, watching old family videos, and pop culture, that I didn't really do or try anything else. But I'm not going to tell Connor that. If this is Connor's way of asking me to go skating with them, I'm not going to tell him no. It just means I'm going to have to teach myself how to skate, so I don't embarrass myself in front of him.

"I love skating!" That sounded completely over the top.

"Awesome! We'll have to go to the rink sometime soon, then. They play the best music." Suddenly, Connor and Greg break out into a song. It isn't until the terrible drum solo they play on their thighs that I realize it's "In the Air Tonight" by Phil Collins. The rest of us can't help but laugh at them.

△△△

The appliance store that CeCe's dad owns is quite impressive. I just thought it was going to be a small Mom and Pop shop, but it's two floors of all kinds of appliances, and TVs. The TVs are lined up to the right of the store in various sizes, some are the biggest I've ever seen. One is half the size of the wall. You would never even have to go to the movies if you owned a TV that size. But I can't picture anyone ever buying a TV that big and bulky. I'm not even sure there's a living room in Noir it could fit in.

CeCe is behind the front counter checking her peachy lipstick through a compact mirror. Valerie is helping a customer choose a washer and dryer set. Both of them wear the same kind of uniform: khaki pants with a purple and green shirt that says, "Daley's Appliances."

I can't wait until the day that my mom and dad say I can go get a job. A lot of kids complain about having to balance their jobs and homework, but I think I'd be able to handle the pressure well. My dream would be to work at a record shop, just like in *Pretty in Pink*.

CeCe tells us that she and Valerie will be ready to go as soon as Valerie closes the deal on the washer and dryer. The rest of the group walks around the store, poking around at all the things. My body is itching to get out and breathe the fresh air, maybe walk around Main Street and take in the sights and sounds.

Connor must sense my need to leave the store because he asks me if I want to take a walk. We step outside, and I instantly feel better. The humidity is a lot stronger now, not as chilly as before, and lightning strikes off in the distance against the dark blue sky. Streetlamps are starting to slowly flicker on. It's not quite dusk, but with the storm that's brewing, it looks and feels a lot later. Hopefully mom doesn't count this as being out after dark.

The buildings that line Main Street all look historic. It's like being taken back through time. A barber shop sits on the corner next to CeCe's dad's store. The red, white, and blue pole is lit up and swirling, signifying the shop is open. Through the big front window, I can see that a man is sitting in the chair, while the barber snips at his thick, brown hair. A bakery is across the street. The smell of the beignets drifts out as a customer leaves. There's a diner that's full of people sitting down for a nice dinner. Cars drive up and down the street as they head to various destinations, some slowing down to find a place to park in front of the buildings.

All these things may seem so normal to everybody else, but to me, watching people go about their everyday lives is like magic. Seeing people living their lives, doing the things they love, discovering things they don't like, it's fascinating to me. I want to bask in the mundane. I want to see the fantastic things. I want to experience life because I spent so long sleeping through it.

"Have you been to Main Street before?" Connor asks, noticing the way I'm watching the people around us.

"No—I mean, yes?"

"The accident?" he asks. I haven't mentioned the accident or coma to Connor, but I'm sure he's heard it from someone. Or maybe he remembers hearing it from the news when I woke up.

Afterall, I was a local celebrity for a minute.

"Yeah. I don't like talking about it too much. It's not really fascinating when you don't know what happened other than waking up in a hospital one day, no longer an eleven-year-old." I reach up and rub my fingers across the pendant at my neck. A nervous habit I've developed since my dad gave it back to me.

"Good luck charm?" Connor eyes the necklace.

"Sort of. I was wearing it the day I was—attacked." Not that I believe in good luck charms, but something kept me safe that day, and it's nice to think that it could have been because of this gift from my dad.

"Ah. It's...interesting. The engraving, I mean. It's unique." Connor rubs his chest.

"I think it must be old. My dad got it from some antique shop." I glance around.

Connor clears his throat. "So, does Noir feel brand new?"

I spin in a circle, taking in the sights of the street, the sound of the rain starting to fall. "It does feel new, and sometimes unsafe, but it still feels like home."

Connor opens his umbrella and pulls me underneath. "Well, I'm glad you're home, Jen." I feel like he may lean in to kiss me, but then Greg knocks into Connor's shoulder from behind.

"You guys ready to pass out some flyers?" Greg squeezes underneath the umbrella. There really isn't a whole lot of room for him. Another group of kids round the corner of the barber shop.

"Hey Greg! Main Street is supposed to be our turf!" one of them shouts. Guess that's our sign to get out of here.

"We're moving!" Greg yells back. "Moira wants to cut through the woods near the bayou. It'll be faster than going around, and maybe we can beat the storm." My dad has taken me to the bayou many times this year for fishing. I know it better than any other place in Noir. But just because I know the bayou does not mean that I feel comfortable going there when it's getting dark. The thought of being in the bayou when it's dark creates a pit of unease inside of me. Enough creatures lurk during the day, but who knows what could be lurking when the sun has been swallowed by storm clouds.

CHAPTER SEVEN

The huge cypress trees block out any potential light left in the sky. Lightning makes the surroundings visible. The crickets are so loud that the first rumble of thunder goes unnoticed. The second rumble moves through my body and stirs a winged animal from the trees. I shiver at the thought of bats being out here. Frogs croak in the distance as the sound of rain patters, echoing all around. The lower parts of the bayou will flood quickly. The clouds are still holding back what I imagine will eventually be a downpour. I'm grateful it hasn't started pouring, yet.

Nobody thought to bring a flashlight because nobody thought we'd be traipsing through the darkness of the bayou. It's up to our adjusting eyes and the occasional flash of the storm to guide our path.

This seems pretty dumb to me. I understand Moira wanting to cut through to make it to our destination sooner, but with the darkness setting in, I don't think it's going to be any quicker than if we had just walked in the big circle to get to Canal Street. And now we're going to have to be extra careful of any critters roaming around. Especially the gators. Oh, and let's not forget that some unknown person is kidnapping kids. The kidnapper could be anywhere!

Like in a dark bayou.

"Moira, I really don't like this." CeCe reads my mind, saying the words I'm too chicken to say. I don't want to be the one labeled the scaredy cat, even though goosebumps line the length of my arms. "Can't we just turn around?" CeCe asks.

"No, we can't turn around. We'll be out of here and onto Canal in no time." Moira's boots crunch over sticks. I really hope Moira is right. This darkness is starting to make me feel claustrophobic, and it's not even pitch black, yet!

Something cold and wet brushes against my hand, and I almost squeal until I feel that it's the brush of someone's fingers against mine. Connor has moved closer to me. "Are you doing okay?" he quietly asks.

"Believe it or not, I love the bayou, but not when it's like this." I shiver.

"A little farther and everything will be fine." Connor's

words are reassuring, and the fact that he seems so brave helps suppress the tingles that want to move up and down my spine. The guys of the group have boxed us girls into a tight moving circle. It's to make us feel safe, and while I do feel a little safer with those three, I also feel hot and stuffy with them invading our space.

A streak of lightning reveals our surroundings. Somebody screams next to me, and instead of our tight circle going into protective mode, we all jump away from each other in surprise. So much for the guys being the brave ones.

"What the heck was that?!" Mark snaps.

"I'm sorry," Mabel whimpers. "It was me. It's just—when the lightning struck, I saw a snake slither in front of me." To some, hearing that a snake was near would be startling, but I know that a snake is the least of our worries, so I can't help but let out a sigh of relief that it was just a snake.

"Can we please agree to not scream anymore until we're out of here?" Mark asks.

Mabel sniffs. "I'm sorry." We trudge ahead, this time spread out, and our shoes all slosh around as the ground becomes softer in the rain.

One...Two...Three...Four...

I count our steps as we go to take my mind off how creepy it is out here. The distraction works for a while until I stumble over a root. I can't feel the ground anymore. My feet go out from under me, and I start to roll down a hill. I grab onto somebody, dragging them down with me. Sticks hit me as I roll, scratching my arms like the nails of a witch. Other debris is shoved into my mouth, while leaves tangle in my hair. The mud is the worst part, though. It coats my body as I travel down, making me feel like a pig in a mud bath.

We hit the bottom of the slope and the air whooshes out of me. Whoever I pulled down with me groans from somewhere nearby. The dark clouds peak through the tops of the looming cypress trees, and I lay there for a moment, watching them swirl. The sound of droplets hitting the water is closer now. Rolling over, I can make out that the bayou is right behind me. If I had gotten a little more momentum, I would have landed right in it.

I quickly scramble away from it, reminded of what lives in those waters, and I turn to look for whoever I dragged down.

"Hey! Are you okay?" I shout. Something shuffles around my left. The silhouette of a person is standing near the edge of the bayou. "Did you get hurt?" I can make out the shape of a girl.

The silhouette looks to be the size of CeCe or Valerie. "Hey, I'm so sorry about pulling you down too. I hope the mud doesn't ruin our clothes." I try wiping the mud from my shirt. I glance at the girl, wondering why she hasn't said anything yet. Did I make her mad? Lightning shines on her face. The eyes of Penelope

Fink stare back at me and I fall to the ground once more.

CHAPTER EIGHT

Penelope Fink is here, in the bayou. I lay on the ground, rain splattering my face, as I try to process how the girl who's been missing could have been here this whole time without anyone's knowledge. I need to get up. I need to ask her questions, but my mind is still spinning. Her family is going to be so happy to know we've found her.

I finally pull myself together and sit up. And I'm alone. I look all around me but there's no sign of Penelope. No silhouette. She's just vanished. I didn't even hear her leave.

Footsteps squish through the mud behind me. I quickly spin my head, expecting to see Penelope, but as the footsteps get closer, Valerie's voice calls out to me. "I heard you calling, but my shoe got stuck in the mud. Are you alright?"

My voice no longer works. Words are no longer computing. Penelope Fink was standing right here.

"That was some fall, that's for sure." Valerie takes my hands, helping up from the mud. "Earth to Jensen?" she waves her hands in front of me, but my mouth will not function. "Did you hit your head?" That's the question that brings me back to life. Did I hit my head again? That would explain why I thought I saw Penelope Fink. My hands move over the scars on my head. My hair is so wet that I can't tell if I'm bleeding or not, but it doesn't feel like I hit my head. No bumps. Nothing throbbing. I don't think I hit my head.

Penelope Fink was not my imagination. She couldn't have been.

Valerie lightly taps the side of my face.

"I'm fine. I—I saw..." How can I tell Valerie who I saw? She came running up to me just a few seconds after I saw Penelope. It's dark out here, but there's no way Valerie couldn't have seen a shadow running away. And yet, she's not bringing it up, so maybe she didn't see anything and I'll only sound ridiculous if I tell her. "Did you—" I trail off again, trying to figure out the right words to say. They aren't coming to me fast enough.

"Did I what?" she asks. The sound of the water splashing behind us takes our attention. The bayou looks inky black, reflecting the dark clouds in its depths. A current moves across its surface, a little too in sync for it to be caused by the storm. A chill creeps up my spine when I think about what lives in the bayou. Gators. I touch the scar on my head again, reminding myself that they never caught the animal that did this to me.

"We better go. It's not safe near the water," I grab Valerie's arm, and we make our way toward the incline we slid down. I can hear the rest of the group at the top, arguing as to whether or not they should come down and find us.

Valerie and I struggle up the slippery slope, pulling at fallen limbs and roots to get us to the top. A hand from above hits my head. I reach to take it. The calloused hand latches on and yanks Valerie and I the rest of the way.

"We were so worried about you guys! We tried calling out to you, but you didn't say anything," CeCe cries. She's definitely the most emotional person I've ever met.

"Well, if you were so worried, why didn't you come down after us?" Valerie wipes at the mud coating her clothes, clearly annoyed. I don't even know if laundering it is going to work to get the mud out. These clothes may just be destined for the dumpster.

"And have us look like you two? No way," Greg retorts. Greg is right. We look awful. Valerie and I can't help the rest of them hand out flyers. We're filthy, and smell like sweat and earth. People would turn us away the second we'd show up on their doorstep, not caring what it is we are trying to do.

"I think it's best if Valerie and I head home," I say, trying not to sound disappointed. I really do want to hang out with the group, and help the missing kids, but I don't want to do it like this. And odds are it'll only be worse when the mud dries.

"It looks like it could downpour at any second. The mud will wash off in no time," Moira responds.

"Downpour? This evening has already been terrible enough. Sorry, but I agree with Jensen." Valerie is still swiping at her clothes.

"Fine," Moira groans. "Go home and clean yourselves up. You both smell sour. We'll see you tomorrow." And with that the rest of the group walks away from us, looking like one big black blob amongst the shadows.

△△△

I take a shower as soon as I get home. When Mom and Dad saw me walk through the front door, they both gave out a cry of shock. Linda just pointed and laughed at me, calling me a mud monster. Little sisters are a test from God, a test that I unfortunately didn't study for. It took all my strength to not throw mud at her.

Mom had me change my clothes in the basement before I

walked through the rest of the house, fearing that it would be hard enough getting the mud out of my clothes let alone the cream-colored carpet.

While I don't always love my short hair, I'm super thankful in this moment. Poor Valerie. I can't even imagine getting this caked-on mud out of her long, blue-black hair. That would be a nightmare. With my hair, not so much. The mud is tough to rinse out, but brushing the residual remnants is not a difficult task when your hair barely reaches your ears.

My family is downstairs watching TV together. I can hear my dad laughing at something on the show they've chosen. We usually watch TV before bed each night as a way to wind down. Normally, I'd go join them as it's still too early for me to go to bed. The clock on my nightstand hasn't even hit eight, yet. But my body is exhausted from the adventure in the bayou and it's calling out to my bed.

Shutting my door to block out the noise of my family, I move to my bed and curl up underneath my fluffy, pink comforter. My eyelids are heavy but, even though I feel tired, my brain will not turn off the memory of Penelope Fink.

Her eyes stare back at me every time I go to close my own. The shock and confusion on her face likely mirrored my own expression at seeing her.

What could she have possibly been doing out there? Is she

hiding in the bayou? Is her kidnapper living in the bayou? Are more of the missing kids out there with her?

So many questions flood my thoughts, and without any answers to quiet them, sleep is going to be next to impossible.

CHAPTER NINE

That was the worst night of sleep I've ever had in my entire life. You would think after being in a deep sleep for four years that missing out on a few hours of shut eye would be no big deal for me. However, the dark circles under my eyes remind me that it most definitely is a big deal.

I had begged my mom to let me use her concealer, but that was a quick no. She insisted that I'm not old enough to wear makeup, but every other girl in school has already been wearing it for years. It does me no good to stomp my feet and complain, though. If I do that then I'm just compared to Linda, which is beyond annoying.

The only option I have is to wear a bright color in order to bring some brightness back into my face. A neon yellow shirt and blue leggings it is. I look like a walking glowstick, but it will at least take the attention away from my raccoon face.

At least I thought it would take the attention away. When Moira and Mabel meet me at my locker this morning, I realize my attempts to cover up my horrible night's rest were futile.

"You look like the walking dead," Moira's gaze travels over me. Of course, Moira looks like a supermodel today. Like freaking Iman herself.

I tug at my messy hairstyle. If you can even call it a "style." It looks like squirrels ran through my hair. "I-uh-bad dreams," I blurt. "They kept me awake. Tossed and turned all night." I slam my locker door, walking away from their gawking eyes.

"Bayou fever," I hear Mabel whisper from behind me, which only makes me pick up my pace.

"No. No way are you walking away." Moira grabs my arm and spins me. Her rich, brown eyes burn into my own. "Spill," Moira demands. My body goes rigid. I think rigor mortis has set into my muscles. How could she possibly know something is bothering me? She barely even knows me! Then again, she's understood me ever since we met. Maybe she has some kind of special intuition. Regardless of what it is, I'm not sure I can talk about what's wrong. I don't know how anyone will feel if I tell them that I saw Penelope with my own two eyes.

"There's nothing to spill, Moira." I shake her hand off my

arm and continue my walk to English.

"You little liar! I can see it in your tired, scared eyes. Just tell me. We're friends, Jen."

I abruptly stop, taking in a shaky breath. I face the concerned faces of Moira and Mabel, hoping that this isn't the last time they'll ever talk to me. "Fine, here's the truth, but just remember that I know what I saw and I'm not losing it." Their wide-eyed expressions turn to each other and then back to me, waiting for the rest of my response. "Last night, in the bayou, I saw—" I lick my lips to help the words slide out of my mouth. Mabel motions for me to go on. "Last night, I saw Penelope."

"WHAT?!" they both exclaim at the same time.

"Was she okay?"

"Did she say anything?"

"When did you see her?"

"I didn't see her. Did anyone else see her?"

Waves of questions are coming at me all at once that I feel like I might drown in them as my chest tightens. "Just—hold on a minute, okay?" I take in a gulp of air as I tell them the whole story. When I finish, it looks like their jaws are going to have to be picked up off the floor.

Moira is the first one to snap out of her stupor. "So, you didn't actually see her then, right? It had to have been your mind playing tricks on you."

"She looked right at me," I counter.

"Wait, Valerie was with you. Did she see Penelope?" Mabel asks.

And this is where my story is going to completely fall apart because I don't think Valerie saw her. "I—don't think so. But it was dark! It was hard for me to even see her until I got close."

"Well, then, where did she disappear to? And why?" Moira shakes her head. "It doesn't make sense."

"You're right. It doesn't make sense, which is exactly why we should be going back out there to look for her again." I don't know why I say that. I shouldn't have said that. I'm scared to go back out there, afraid of what else we might find, but I can't shake the feeling that there are more answers in the bayou.

"Alright, tonight. Let's do it," Moira says.

I shake my head. "Sorry, can't. I promised Connor we'd research our project for Mr. C's class at the library tonight."

"Ooh, like a date?" Mabel gets excited.

"No—not—I don't think it's a date," I stammer.

Mabel and Moira both begin to laugh. Moira manages to pull herself together. "Oh, it's a date. At least in Connor's eyes. That boy is so smitten by you. Although, you should definitely try to freshen up before. Can't be looking like death on the first date."

I roll my eyes, groaning at the two of them. But their words begin to sink in, and a swarm of butterflies invade my stomach. What if Connor really does think this is a date? And I woke up today looking the worst I ever have! Rocks suddenly rain down inside me, squashing all the butterflies. Fingers crossed he doesn't think I look awful and call off the whole thing. But maybe that would be better?

ΔΔΔ

The library is beautiful. Ornate ceilings with intricate lights hanging from them create an elegant atmosphere. Glossy, smooth desks are spaced throughout, with many people reading and writing at them. The chairs match the wood of the desks and have navy blue cushions for comfort. Aisles and aisles of bookcases fill in the rest of the space, the Dewey Decimal system placed at the end of each row.

A young woman sits behind the front desk, stamping books in that have been dropped off by patrons. She doesn't look like the librarians depicted on TV or in movies. No, she's much more fashionable. Her pale blue cardigan is paired with a cute white button-up with flowers that match. Brown hair, that matches her brown eyes, is pulled up into a high-ponytail, and her bangs are teased to perfection. The sweep of light blue eyeshadow on her eyelids completes her look.

Connor and I stand at the front desk, his fingers tapping on the counter. He picked me up from my house, which makes it feel even more like a date, but maybe I'm still reading too much into it. He didn't even dress up, whereas I look incredibly overdressed in my burgundy dress, matching shawl, and platform wedges. I should have never listened to Moira. She recommended I wear something eye catching. I look completely impractical standing next to Connor.

I've been trying not to think about it too much, this whole thing being a date, because every time I do, I feel like I'm going to lose my dinner. It didn't help that my dad, in typical dad form, asked Connor a thousand questions before he would even let us leave. I felt like passing out from embarrassment when he went as far as suggesting he *drive* us to the library instead of Connor.

My fingers itch to caress the pendant around my neck, but I don't want Connor to know how anxious I am. While I may be nervous about being here with Connor, I'm also excited. The electric feeling of exhilaration is humming inside of me, and not just because of Connor. The library has me in complete awe. I haven't read an actual book since I've come home. Most of my reading has consisted of textbooks and teen gossip magazines. But I feel so happy in this space right now that I wonder if I once loved reading books just because. Did I ever read about the high-seas adventure in *Moby Dick*? Would horror stories like *Dracula* keep me up at night?

"Can I help you two?" the librarian asks. Her name tag says Donna.

"We're looking for books on Mythology and Folklore. Could you point us in the right direction?" Connor asks.

Donna picks up another book and stamps it. "Give me one second and I'll check the catalog for you." She looks a little annoyed that she has to stop what she's doing to help us. Her heels click across the floor as she moves toward the card catalog. I guess Connor and I could have flipped through the catalog, but I don't know the first thing about using one.

"Here are some book titles and authors that cover that subject. You'll find most of them in section three-hundred and ninety-eight."

"Thank you," Connor says, and we make our way to the correct section.

There's a lot of books revolving around the subjects of Mythology and Folklore. Connor already has his hands full with books covering topics on Folklore and Myths. I, on the other hand, read spine after spine of book titles, none of them sticking out to me.

Connor scans the books I've been staring at, his books starting to teeter. I take the top half from him, so they don't go crashing to the ground. "Thanks for that." He grins wide enough for his dimple to appear. "This looks like a good start. Why don't we find a table and get to work?" Connor nudges me with his elbow. I hadn't exactly picked any books out, but he had grabbed enough for the both of us.

We empty our arms onto an unoccupied table and begin our journey down the rabbit hole of cryptids. I choose a book titled *Monsters of the South* which sounds promising to me, but as the clock moves on the wall, and I flip through page after page, I'm not getting any hits. Nothing seems to stick out. The next book I try from our pile is called *Werewolves Among Us.* Sounds quite unbelievable to me, and yet it's filed in the Non-Fiction section.

I want to make a joke about it to Connor, but he is completely engrossed in whatever book he's reading, frantically taking notes. I didn't even bring a notebook. Then again, I didn't think we'd actually be doing much studying. My teenage brain thought this was going to be our opportunity to get to know more about each other, and maybe get a quick study in so it looked like we accomplished something. Joke's on me.

Training my eyes back on the book in front of me, I shut the part of my brain off that desperately wants this to be a date and put on my study face. Story after story of werewolves being spotted in various parts of the world. All of them bear a different name. Werewolf. Lycanthrope. Loup Garou. Rougarou. Shapeshifter.

The legends all sound similar. A person who can transform into a wolf or hybrid creature of man and wolf. Some can transform on command, while others require the shadow of night or the light of a full moon to transform. And no silver bullets. No, that was added for Hollywood. The werewolves in these stories must be stabbed through the heart or else they continue to be blood thirsty beasts searching for the next victim. Some of the stories talk about special objects used to control the creatures. Wolfsbane is an object of protection, while magic blessed trinkets can be used to control and even kill them.

Goose bumps race up my body and I pull my shawl tighter.

"Are you cold?" Connor scoots closer, his body heat and concern instantly making me warmer.

"Oh, I—I think the air conditioning just kicked on." I wasn't about to tell him that this book was giving me chills. He drapes one arm over the back of my chair and goes back to his book. My insides are gushing at the gesture, however small it is, and I feel like I might explode. This is the kind of stuff that happens in movies and has every girl swooning. Okay, maybe I'm being a little over the top, but I'd like to think if this were a movie the audience would be saying "aw" right about now.

No longer feeling chilled, I shut the book and pick up a

new one. This one is titled *Shapeshifted*, which sounds a lot lighter than *Monsters Among Us*. The first few chapters are big dull duds that I quickly skim through. It mostly discusses how shapeshifters have been in existence for years and can be the explanation behind a number of cryptids and monsters people see. Vampires, Bigfoot, The Loch Ness Monster are potentially shapeshifters, able to make themselves into humans, thus the reason behind the rare sightings. I don't find any of these cryptids interesting.

As I go to close this book and move onto the next, a paper slips out from the pages. It's not a part of the book. I half expect the piece of paper to be a grocery list or scrap that was used as a makeshift bookmark, but I flip it over and see that it's clearly notes someone had taken, probably using this book as a guide for the scribbles haphazardly made across the paper.

-full moon

-missing children

-shifter

-letiche: born of the devil, raised by----

The rest of the words are too smudged to make out, but at the bottom of the page is a cartoon sketch of an alligator. Maybe some type of weird signature? I shove the paper back into the book and hold it to my chest, thinking the words over in my head and what they could mean.

"Something on your mind?" Connor's finger brushes against my arm, making me jump.

"Do you know what Letiche means?" I don't even know if I'm pronouncing it right, but I'm hoping he knows what I'm trying to say.

"Oh," Connor looks surprised for some reason. "It's one of the cryptids centered around Louisiana."

"It's a cryptid?" I ask. I just thought it was some fancy French word.

"Yeah? Isn't it in that book you're holding?" Connor raises an eyebrow. If I wouldn't have gotten distracted by the paper, I would have been able to find that out.

"Right... but it—the book is vague about it. Do you know anything that maybe the book doesn't say?" I'm fumbling over my words trying to make it appear like I at least read some of the book.

"The Letiche is a cryptid that lives in the swamps of Louisiana, but it's been spotted in other Southern states." Connor has a distant look. "They say it's the child of the devil. Some legends say that a spirit possessed a child and fled to the swamps. Other legends say it was a creature summoned by the Natives. I tend to believe the latter."

"What makes you believe that?"

"Oh, just a...personal opinion," Connor fidgets with his

fingers.

"Where do the legends come from?" I ask.

"Locals. People who live on the bayou. I would imagine that it's a popular story among people our grandparents' age."

"It's that old of a story?" I laugh.

Connor smiles. "It's a very historical story. Part of Louisiana's forgotten history. I think it's told to scare kids into staying out of the bayou."

"And the Letiche would be in a book about shapeshifters because....?"

"Because there have been many sightings of gators shifting into human form to walk amongst society, luring people back to the swamps to cure their thirst for blood." Connor waggles his fingers in front of me to add to the creepy tale.

"And the Letiche is an alligator?" That would answer the scribbles on the page.

Born of the devil, raised by—

Alligators.

Connor nods his head, answering my question. I gulp loudly. "Did my story scare you?" he asks with a devilish grin.

I laugh. "You paint a lovely tale, but no. I'm not scared senseless. Actually, I think you just helped me find my cryptid for the project."

CHAPTER TEN

After the "kind of" date at the library with Connor, the thought of Penelope Fink had completely left my mind. I had a good night's rest, no nightmares of Penelope's ghostly face in the bayou, and a great weekend of fishing with my dad. Then Moira brought it up again on Monday, and it all came flooding back.

"We meet tonight at my house and then we go to the bayou to find Penelope." Moira was laying the plan out for us at lunch. Since Connor doesn't have lunch at the same time as the rest of us, it'll be my job to fill him in after Mythology.

My stomach is in knots thinking about going back to the bayou. What if we don't find Penelope out there tonight? What if I imagined the whole thing and I end up being labelled the high-school weirdo? Being weird worked out for Ally Sheedy's character in *The Breakfast Club*, but I doubt I have that kind of luck.

"Oh, and don't forget flashlights!" Moira points to all of us and everyone laughs, remembering how awful it was the other night without flashlights. I halfheartedly join in on the laughter, still feeling unsure. I hate second guessing myself, especially when I had felt so positive about seeing her, but I guess that's what happens when you've been able to overthink things for a few days.

In Mythology, Mr. C is eagerly awaiting our written responses as to what cryptid we've chosen for our essays. I had written mine as soon as Connor dropped me off at home on Friday. It just had to be a quick response; one paragraph on the cryptid we've chosen and why. Part of our assignment today is to get up in front of the class and read our responses. Mr. C randomly draws names from a hat. We're supposed to have at least three cryptids written down in case someone has already chosen the same one. I've only written one, though, as I'm fairly confident that nobody else will be picking the Letiche.

"Jensen Swells, you're up." Mr. C tosses the scrap of paper with my name on it in the trash. A rush of nerves goes through my body, but Connor gives me an encouraging smile that helps me feel like I'm not going to throw up. At least not right now.

I clear my throat, hoping to prevent my voice from

cracking when I speak. The folder that contains my scribbled paragraph, the handwriting resembling something my little sister would write, feels like it's going to slip from my shaking hands as I hold it open. Mr. C props himself up against the heat register that lines the walls in front of me. His t-shirt is tucked into his khaki pants. The shirt reads "Save the Cryptids" in black lettering. How very fitting.

"After researching many cryptids, from Bigfoot to the Jersey Devil, none of them piqued my interest. Then I stumbled upon the legend of the Letiche." I look up at the class to see if that name rings any bells. All blank, bored stares. The only person who seems remotely interested in what I've just said is Mr. C. His eyes are wide in surprise. As the Mythology teacher, I assume he must be familiar with this legend.

I continue. "The Letiche is relative to southern states, but more specifically Louisiana, where it hides itself amongst the alligators that frequent the bayou." Folding my paper back up, I hand it in to Mr. C and make my way back toward my seat. A slow clap echoes across the classroom as my peers finally act like they're awake. They probably have no idea what I even said and don't care what my essay is going to be on anyway. It's not their grade.

Connor gives me a thumbs up. I'm glad at least he enjoyed what little I had to say.

"Great job, Jensen." Mr. C walks to the front of the class, taking a seat on his desk like it somehow makes him cooler. "The Letiche is a very interesting choice indeed. I look forward to your research and your stance on the subject." He places his glasses on his desk and calls the next victim... I mean student.

The rest of class passes by in a blur. Student after student naming cryptid after cryptid and then doing the walk of shame back to their desk. Afterwards, I inform Connor of the evening plans that Moira has put together.

"We'll need to bring flashlights, but it shouldn't be as dark this time. There's a full moon tonight."

"Oh, yeah. A full moon..." Connor sounds disconcerted.

"I promise there's no werewolves out there," I laugh. At least I hope there's no werewolves.

Connor smiles, seeming less nervous and more excited now. "We'll be like the Scooby gang," he says with a wink.

Convincing my mom about this evening is way harder than expected.

"Absolutely not." She chops through a pepper with force. Jambalaya must be on the menu tonight. "It's a school night."

"I'll be home before my own bedtime," I protest.

"Do you honestly think, after everything you've been through, that I'm going to let you go wandering through the bayou with a group of your friends who, by the way, I have never met?"

"We'll be safe. I promise." She doesn't know that we already went through the bayou once in the dark. "It's not like the Letiche is going to get us." I roll my eyes.

She raises an eyebrow. "What did you say?"

"I—nothing." Maybe the Letiche isn't something my grandparents ever talked about, but if they did, I don't want to give my mom another reason not to let me go to the bayou.

"How can you promise you will be safe when the bayou is unpredictable?" While she isn't wrong about the bayou, I know that the odds of something bad happening to me a second time have to be slim. There's no way I'm a magnet for all things terrible. I deserve some good luck every now and then. Thankfully, I don't have to argue my point, because Dad walks through the kitchen door, lab coat in hand, and automatically detects our tension. He always seems to know when Mom and I are having a disagreement, and he's always the one to come to my defense. Fingers crossed I can win him to my side once again.

"And what's going on here?" he asks, needing the details of the argument.

"Pete, please tell our daughter that, no, she cannot go frogging with her friends in the bayou tonight." Mom rubs the bridge of her nose. Frogging is the excuse I gave as to why we would be out in the bayou tonight. It's not like I can tell them the truth. 'Oh, my friends and I are going to look for a girl who was kidnapped that I think I saw in the bayou.' I could just imagine my mom's brain exploding all over the floor.

"Frogging, huh?" Dad grins. I knew he would eat the frogging thing right up. He loves that his little girl is into all that kind of stuff. According to him, before the accident, I was his fishing partner, hunting partner, frogging partner, etcetera. He told me all about how he didn't even have to teach me how to bait a hook. After so many times watching him do it, I was able to do it myself by the time I was four. Apparently, my love for all those things stuck with me even after I woke up.

He'll be helping me pack a net before I can count to ten. "I think that's awesome! A group of you are going?"

Five seconds. Record time.

"Yeah. I guess it's what some of the highschoolers like to do. A way to let loose." I feel a slight pang in my chest about lying, but it dissipates when I remind myself that without the little white lie, I may be locked up in my house forever. Then again, I might be locked up forever if my mom finds out I'm lying. It's a risk I'm willing to take.

"And this is probably the exact reason kids have been going missing. It'd be irresponsible for us to let her go out there, especially on a school night." My mom glares at my dad.

"Catie, she'll be with a group. Let her have some fun with

the kids her own age. Home before ten though, okay?"

I leap for joy and wrap my dad in a hug. Mom huffs out a breath of annoyance. She'll definitely be giving Dad an earful the second I leave. "Thanks, Dad! I'll be home before the clock strikes ten!"

Zooming out of the kitchen to go to my room, I bump right into Linda, knocking the little brat on her butt. "Ouch! That hurt, Jen!"

Normally, I would just leave her on the floor, but feeling in a good mood, I help her up. "Sorry about that. Just a little excited."

"Excited for what?" she snaps.

"I'm going to hang out with some friends in the bayou tonight." I walk past her to the stairs, listening to her wail into the kitchen.

"I wanna go to the bayou tonight!"

I snicker at her whining, thankful for the age gap we have. I can't imagine having a sibling my own age that I'd have to share everything with. The little things Mom makes Linda and I share already is enough to drive me crazy.

I'm sure our parents thought that we would become best friends one day, and maybe at one time that was true. The time before the accident when I played with her, turning her into a mini me according to my mom. Those times are long gone, and now neither of us want to build a close sibling bond. I wish I could say it's all her fault, but I know the truth.

Things have been hard since coming home and both of us have been incredibly territorial of our parents, personal possessions, and the house. I think it hurt Linda that I had no memory of her or the times we had when I came back. Being the older sister, it's probably my job to fix the relationship, but Linda can be such a monster sometimes that it's just not worth it.

I throw on a plain gray t-shirt and tie a sweater around my waist. I choose some muck boots for footwear, tucking my jeans tightly into them. While we aren't really frogging, the only sensible shoes to ever wear in the bayou are muck boots. Unless you're Moira, who will probably be wearing whatever shoes were last seen on the cover of Vogue.

My hair sticks up in all different directions. It tends to do this when it's humid outside, and after the last couple days of rain, the humidity has returned with a vengeance. A hairstyle like this on a model looks intentional, but on me it looks like I just got electrocuted. Plopping a Breton hat on top of my head covers up my unruly pixie, even though it doesn't exactly look right with my boots.

I don't feel one hundred percent confident in my outfit when I first put it on, but we'll be slopping around in the mud and dark. I start to feel a lot better about my choice in outfit when Connor tells me I look cute. The amount of warmth that reaches my cheeks is unreal when he says it. To my surprise, Moira is wearing sensible shoes. Not muck boots, but boots, nonetheless. I guarantee they're still designers.

"Everybody got their flashlights?" Greg taps his flashlight in his hand, testing the batteries within it.

My dad, wanting me to have a successful frogging night, packed my backpack full of gear. At first, I was a little embarrassed about lugging all this stuff around with me, but Moira and CeCe have backpacks on just as big and full as mine. I have snacks, nets, and two collapsible frog gigs.

Outside is sticky. Bugs buzz all around, and mosquitos get ready to feast on us. The crickets, frogs, and other creatures that call the bayou home create a cacophony all around, the noise echoing off the trees. It's a deafening noise that takes a moment for my ears to adjust.

The sun is almost gone, the sky a dark blue as grey clouds move in. The weather was supposed to be clear for the night, but Louisiana showers this time of year can be unpredictable. One minute it could be fine, the next it could rain for ten days straight.

It's a good thing we didn't decide to rely on the light from the full moon tonight. I don't think it'll be out too much with the clouds moving in.

Every crack of a branch, splash of water, slosh of mud, and rustle of leaves has my body on edge. The noises keep me on my toes as I anticipate each sound being Penelope wandering around.

"Penelope?" Mabel calls out, her voice timid.

Moira waves her flashlight around. "Penelope!" Moira isn't afraid to shout her name louder. Her shouting makes me a little uncomfortable. Anything—or anyone—could respond to her call.

"Maybe we should be a little more subtle?" I suggest. CeCe and Valerie just roll their eyes at me.

"The sooner we can find Penelope, the sooner we get out of here, Jen." Moira is right, but I still don't feel good about it. Sweat starts to build up under my arms. I regret choosing to wear a grey shirt. I just hope no one can see it under the light of their flashlights.

"You saw her near the water, right? Down the embankment?" Mark asks.

"I mean, it was after we fell, so yeah. And she was near the edge of the water, but that doesn't mean she'll be there again," I say.

"But maybe she'd go back there," Greg suggests.

"We should probably split up." Connor looks at me to see if I agree.

"That's a good idea." Even if we don't find Penelope, it'd be a good opportunity for Connor and me to spend some more time together.

"Alright, me, Mabel, Connor and Jen will take the woods. Greg, Mark, CeCe, and Val you guys go take near the water." Moira goes deeper into the woods before anyone else can respond to her. So much for spending more alone time with Connor. There is a slight relief, though, to know we'll be walking around the woods instead of near the bayou.

Our flashlights guide our path through the dark cypress trees. Hours tick by as we slosh through the moist ground and jump at every sound. My legs are growing tired from all the walking, and with no sign of Penelope, I want to just admit that maybe I was wrong and go home.

Moira, sounding a little annoyed, beats me to it. "This is useless. I think you saw someone or something else out here, Jensen. Let's find the others and get out of here."

The only thoughts that cross my mind are ones that involve everyone never speaking to me again. Sure, it wasn't my idea to drag them all out into the bayou on some wild goose chase, but I was the one who told them about Penelope.

Connor brushes a thumb over my elbow as if to reassure me that everything is fine. I give him a small smile, hoping that in the darkness he can't make out the tears I'm trying to hold back.

We wander over to the embankment, about to make our way down toward the bayou, when my flashlight hovers over pale skin and brown, messy hair. Penelope.

ONE POT JUMPIN' JAMBALAYA

What you'll need:

13.5 oz Andouille sausage

2 chicken breasts, cooked and shredded

1 bell pepper, sliced

1 yellow onion, sliced

1 cup frozen okra

1 14.5 oz can diced tomatoes and juices

1 8 oz can of tomato sauce

2 cups chicken or vegetable broth

1.5 cups of white rice, uncooked and rinsed

1 tsp paprika

½ tsp garlic powder

½ tsp onion powder

¼ - ½ tsp cayenne pepper

1 tsp Cajun seasoning

½ tsp kosher salt

1 tbsp olive oil

Directions:

Slice the sausage into quarter sized rounds and set aside. In a large pot or Dutch oven, add olive oil, peppers, and onions. Sauté over medium heat until they become soft and onions start to turn translucent. Add in sausage and stir. Continue sauteing until sausage starts to brown (sausage is precooked, so this step doesn't take long). Add in shredded chicken, rice, and spices and stir to combine. Add in broth, tomato sauce, diced tomatoes, and frozen okra. Stir. Bring to a boil and cover and reduce heat to simmer. Cook, covered, for 15-20 minutes or until rice is tender. Watch closely and stir occasionally to prevent rice from browning or sticking to the bottom.

CHAPTER ELEVEN

When our gazes meet, Penelope runs off deeper into the woods, but I'm not going to lose her this time. I run after her, hearing the shouts of my friends behind me. She's a lot faster than I am, easily maneuvering around the slick terrain, but I'm determined. I'll follow her all night if I have to.

Running in muck boots is no easy task, and before I know it, I trip over my own feet, landing hard on the ground. I know there's no way I'll catch her now. Sitting up, I slap the ground and scream in frustration. I was so *close!*

The trees move, rustled by wind. Faint light from the full moon trying to peek through the clouds casts shadows. Penelope's footsteps can't be heard. A hissing growl from the darkness penetrates my ears. Eyes that I can't see but can feel are watching me from somewhere. They burn into me. Something moves over the mud. I can hear the ground squishing under its feet. The shrubbery shakes in the dark and I know it's not the wind. Panic seizes in my chest, but I can't move. I'm frozen in my vulnerable spot on the ground.

Penelope runs out of the darkness, as silent as a mouse. "You have to get out of here!" She's frantic, but I'm still frozen, my limbs not wanting to work. "Please!" she pleads, looking toward the trees behind us. I finally snap out of it.

"Penelope, you have to come with me. Everyone's been looking for you." I get off the ground, not taking my eyes off her.

She shakes her head. "I can't leave, Jensen." I'm taken aback. I have no idea how she could possibly know my name. We've never met personally.

"What? I don't understand. Your family misses you. Your friends miss you. We've been looking for you all night."

She gives a sad smile. "I know. But I can't leave here." And to show me what she means, she reaches out and touches me, her pale hand moving right through my body, leaving a cold chill in its wake. A wild sound bubbles out of me as uncontrollable giggles erupt from my lips.

This can't be real. I must be imagining what just happened. I have to be dreaming. I pinch myself, hard. The sting of it moves across my arm, and snaps my brain into focus. This is no dream. I'm wide awake.

A wave of nausea rolls through me as I realize what this means. Penelope is dead. A ghost haunting the bayou.

Penelope's eyes fill with fear, her voice becoming urgent. "Leave. The bayou isn't safe anymore."

I want to protest—to stay and figure out a way to help her, and maybe find out what exactly happened to her—but I'm in shock.

A twig cracks somewhere nearby. Penelope glances into the dark woods, her eyes shifting up to the now exposed golden light of the full moon. *"Run,"* she harshly whispers, and then vanishes right before my eyes. I'm smart enough to know that if a ghost looks that terrified and is telling me to run then I better get my feet moving.

Muck boots slapping against the ground, I run for my life, although, I'm not entirely sure what from, but I feel like I'm being stalked by something. The feeling of powerlessness floods my body as terror grows in me. What if it catches me? What if I end up as a ghost—just like Penelope.

I run harder.

The beam of my flashlight bounces around, casting menacing shadows that seem to move with me. Pumping my legs as my lungs wheeze, my chest on fire, I try to push through the burn, reminding myself that I can't get caught.

My footing falters a little when I take a sharp turn. I regain my balance, but the slip up is just enough for the danger in the bayou to make a move. Arms wrap around my waist and I start swinging. All of my appendages rage against the person holding me who reeks of putrid body odor. The rotten smell fills my nostrils and leaves an acrid taste in the back of my throat, turning my stomach. Kicking at the stranger doesn't seem to be doing anything. Clawing at the arms squeezing around my waist has no effect. I use the one part of my body that's left open, and I know I'm going to regret it later.

I use my head like a wrecking ball and bash it against the chin that's over my shoulder. Stars float in front of me, pain crackling across my skull. I silently pray that I don't pass out, that the scars on my head aren't jarred to the point that my skull comes apart. Is that even possible?

The stranger behind me grunts as warmth spreads across my head, dripping onto my shoulders. This is the one time that I hope it's my blood. The thought of a stranger's blood covering me mixes queasiness with the adrenaline that's already surging through my veins.

The grip on my waist loosens and I break free, quickly turning to face my attacker. The woods spin around me even though I'm standing still. I feel unsteady. Heads aren't supposed to be used as weapons, especially not heads that have suffered injuries before.

The stranger before me is a man in tattered clothing. His hair, what hair he has, is just wisps of white and black greasy strands that don't cover his whole head. A toothless grin, made menacing by the blood dripping from his nose, makes me stumble backwards as I try to create more distance between us.

The man spits a clot of blood and it lands on the ground in front of him. I dig my nails into my palms to keep myself from passing out. "You shouldn't be here. Little girls don't last long in the bayou." He takes a step closer and that's all the fuel I need to start running again. I start to panic when I realize that I've dropped my flashlight, and the moon is now under the clouds again. I say a silent prayer that my feet will magically know where to go.

I'm not an athletic person at all. The coma made sure my body would never be able to handle any intense physical exertion over long periods of time. There are never going to be track coaches or soccer coaches fighting over me because none of my muscles truly work properly. Though right now, with the mud flying up behind me, I bet I'd get every single sports team's attention. I'd probably have colleges begging for me to grace their hallways, offering me full rides on my running alone.

Everything hurts like crazy. My body is screaming at me to stop, but the thought of what could happen to me if I do stop is too terrifying. If he's the one who's been kidnapping kids, the one who killed Penelope, I have to get as far away as I can.

A body slams into me, stealing my breath as I fall to the ground screaming. I kick and claw at the person now lying on top of me. I will not make my death easy for him.

"Ouch!" The pained voice of Connor pulls me from my savagery. He gets off me and I'm already grabbing his arm and dragging him along with me. He's trying to shake me off the whole way. His protests reach my ears, but I block them out. I won't let anything happen to either of us. When I think we're far enough away, I pull us into a shrouded area so we can catch our breath.

Scratches from my nails tearing into him mar his gorgeous face. His shirt and shorts are slightly torn. Did I do that? I don't think it's possible that I could have torn his clothes. I didn't think I was that crazed, but maybe I truly did go overboard. "Connor—" the look of horror on my face must be apparent because his eyes are so gentle, like I'm a gazelle, and he could frighten me away at any second.

I. Want. To. Disappear.

I shrivel under his gaze. He reaches out to me, but then pulls his arms back down to his sides. He's unsure of what to think of me right now. I don't blame him.

"What happened? You're shaking all over." He's right. I'm

trembling. Adrenaline is dissipating and embarrassment sets in. Then I remember what Penelope had said and how scared she was, and the way the man grabbed me and squeezed me in his arms, his wicked grin full of blood making me queasy.

"There's a man—he—he grabbed me. I think he has something to do with Penelope. We need to get out of here."

"Is that your blood?" He points to the blood on my shoulder. It's become so dark that it almost blends in with the mud on my clothes. I'm surprised he can even tell that it's blood.

"It's not mine. I promise."

Connor looks confused, but we don't have the time for me to stand here and explain every single detail of what happened to him. I'm kind of glad I don't have to do that right now. I need to process everything that's happened to me tonight before I go spilling my guts to the rest of the group.

"Where are the others?" I march off in the direction where Connor had come from, him following closely behind.

"They're not too far behind. They went to round everyone up after you took off. I separated to come find you."

I fidget with my necklace. The familiar shape of the pendant calms my nerves.

Connor reaches for the hand at my neck but stops himself from touching me. His voice sounds concerned. "Jen, what—"

I cut him off. "Not now, Connor. We need to go."

Moira and the others come jogging up to us. "Holy crap, Jen. You scared us all to death, taking off into the woods like that! Don't ever do that again," Moira shakes me.

Looking around, I notice that not everyone is here. "Where is CeCe?" I ask, moving past Moira, heart fluttering in my chest.

"She got freaked out down by the bayou, said she was going home. I walked her back to the road," Greg says, trying to ease my worry, but my stomach still feels like a bunch of bees are buzzing around in it.

Moira loops her arm through mine. "I think we should all go home. This place is giving me the absolute creeps now." And I couldn't agree with Moira more.

Everyone chats with each other about what a bust tonight was, but I can't join in with their conversation.

We all part ways from where we came in. It might not be the best idea for us to be alone, but at least we're all out of the bayou.

Thoughts of calling the police and telling my parents about the strange man swim around my head in circles as I walk home. Someone needs to look into who he is. Those thoughts are quickly replaced by the memory of Penelope's ghostly touch, and the warning she gave. *The bayou isn't safe anymore.*

CHAPTER TWELVE

"She never made it home!" Valerie's makeup streaks down her face, highlighting the tracks of tears. Turns out, after our night in the bayou Monday, CeCe never came home. Her parents are worried sick about her. Valerie is inconsolable. The rest of the group is in shock. CeCe's parents filed the missing person's report Tuesday night. They assumed she had spent the night with Valerie and didn't find out until Tuesday afternoon that that wasn't the case.

"It's all my fault," Moira stares off into space, completely distraught. "If I hadn't made you guys go out there—CeCe," a sob stops her sentence. Guilt stabs me. If I hadn't mentioned Penelope, we would have never been out there.

I wonder how long it will take them to put CeCe's picture

on a milk carton. My eyes mist over. I look down at everyone's uneaten lunches, trying to keep myself from letting the tears leak out.

Greg wipes his nose. "I never should have let her walk home by herself. I should have left with her." I think about the hands that were wrapped around my waist. Did that man have something to do with CeCe's disappearance? It seems a little too coincidental for him not to be connected somehow. The guilt squirms inside of me. I should have said something about him that night.

Valerie cries harder.

"I—" it's hard for me to tell them now, but I force my nerves down and let the words slip past them. "I should have said something sooner. I should have said something that night, but there was a man out there in the bayou. He—he grabbed me." I can still feel his grimy body against me, holding me tight. Everyone at the table stares at me. Mark looks like his jaw is dislocated by how far it's dropped.

Mabel clenches her jaw. "You mean to tell me some random man was out there and you didn't tell us about it?"

"I told Connor, but I was in shock. My only thoughts were on us getting safely out of the bayou."

"Well not all of us made it out safely, Jensen," there's venom in Mabel's voice.

"Wait, what did this man look like?" Moira asks. I describe the man to them and their faces go from mad that I didn't say anything to looks of relief and disappointment. "That's just Al," Moira says his name like I should know exactly who she's talking about. My face must tell her I'm clueless because she continues. "He lives out there, a harmless hermit who used to work for the police department back in the day. My mammy went to school with him."

"So, not a suspect?" I ask. They all shake their heads. I'm still skeptical, but I don't have any time to voice my skepticism before the blame game starts again, Valerie releasing her accusations on Greg for not walking CeCe home.

The guilt I had now turns to anger. We're all sitting here blaming ourselves, blaming each other, when the blame should be placed on whoever is taking these kids. "Guys, it's no one's fault. How were we supposed to know? It could have been anyone of us."

"It should have been *none* of us," Mabel seethes. "But no, you just had to go spewing stories about Penelope. What, being coma girl just wasn't enough attention for you?" Mabel pushes up from the table and storms out of the cafeteria, Mark following close behind.

Valerie sniffs, taking a tissue that Moira offers. "Yeah, you and Moira both just had to play detective. Penelope isn't living in the bayou!" Valerie hiccups.

I watch as Moira's posture changes from defeated to defensive, her shoulders tightening. I don't need Moira yelling at me too. "Listen, I *saw* Penelope out there. And I know why none of you did," I clamp a hand over my mouth, regretting that I even spoke those words out loud. I probably sound ridiculous enough to them as it is.

"And why didn't we see Penelope?" Greg asks.

Too late for me to keep my mouth shut now. "Because —because she's a ghost," I blurt. I'm equal parts horrified and relieved that it's out in the open.

"Oh, so now you can see ghosts?" Greg sounds incredulous, and I don't really blame him.

"Well—I mean, I can see Penelope's ghost. I haven't noticed any other...ghosts... that I know of." They're all looking at me like I have ten heads.

Valerie slaps her hands on the table and walks off with her tissue in hand. Greg rolls his eyes at me and follows Valerie. I'm starting to think I'm going to be left at this lunch table alone, but Moira scoots next to me.

"You don't think I'm lying?" I ask.

"My mammy is sensitive to things. She once said that she knew my grandpa was happy, in a better place, after he passed away. I never questioned her on how she knew that. I've just always believed her." Moira picks at her nails. "Did—did Penelope say anything to you?"

"She told me that the bayou isn't safe anymore."

Moira purses her lips. "So, do you think something is killing kids in the bayou?"

The air around us suddenly feels cold. "It would explain why Penelope's spirit is still out there. I imagine she's staying behind so she can warn people."

"But you're the only one who can see her."

"I almost died in the accident. Maybe I opened up a door inside myself through that experience. Maybe she's stayed behind because she somehow knew I'd find her." Which is exactly why I have to go back into the bayou. It freaks me out going back so soon, but CeCe is missing. I don't know if it's too late to save her, but it's not too late to save somebody else.

"We have to find out what's happening," Moira's voice is determined.

"We will. But we're going to need Penelope's help."

ΔΔΔ

"I just need you to come with me to distract my dad," I say under my breath to Connor as I sit on his desk. Mythology and Folklore will be starting soon, but I need to talk to Connor about everything before the bell rings.

He doesn't seem the least bit concerned when I tell him that I can see ghosts—or at least *a* ghost. He also doesn't seem surprised that CeCe is missing. How could he, though, when that's all anyone seems to be talking about today.

"What do ghosts look like? Is it like something out of a horror movie?" he asks.

"Penelope just looks tired, and cold."

"Wait, did Penelope say who did it? Who killed her?" Connor's shoulders stiffen. There are a lot of questions for me to answer before I can go into detail about my plan.

"So, we go on a fishing excursion with your dad, and I distract him while you go talk to Penelope?" he asks, and I shake my head. There's no way my parents will be on board with me going into the bayou on a school night again. And I'm not sure I can handle going back in the dark right now anyway. The best option will be to ask my dad if he'll go fishing with Connor and I tomorrow after school. Connor will chat with my dad while I get information from Penelope.

"Sounds like a date," Connor winks. Ugh. I think I'm in love. I can hear the wedding bells now.

Nope. That's the actual bell.

Sliding off Connor's desk, I slink down into my own, waiting for Mr. C to start his lesson on Sasquatch. Yippee.

He drones on and on about Sasquatch sightings, and how Sasquatch, Bigfoot, and the Yeti are all from the same species of cryptid. I find myself tuning out most of what he's saying as I think about CeCe, Penelope, and the bayou. I take *Shapeshifted* out of my backpack, glad I put it in there this morning, and flip to the page containing the scribbled-on scrap of paper.

-full moon

-missing children

-shifter

-letiche: born of the devil, raised by----

These words must mean something. They were important enough for somebody to write them down.

Full moon. I write *werewolf connection?* on the note. I wonder if maybe somebody else had the same school assignment and wrote about the Letiche.

Born of the devil, raised by----

I know that the Letiche was raised by alligators, so I write that next to the note. My eyes scan back to the book, looking for anything about the Letiche, but it just discusses the various shapeshifter beliefs throughout the country. The bell rings, startling me, and I knock the book onto the floor.

"First drafts are due next Wednesday, so I suggest you all get started on those very soon," Mr. C announces as we all gather our things to leave. It's bad enough having to worry about talking to a ghost, but I also have to worry about how I'm going to get this essay done on top of it.

Mr. C picks my book off the floor, staring at the cover, a glint in his eyes. I take it from him as politely as I can and shove it back into my backpack. "Learning anything interesting?" he asks, looking at my backpack where the book now resides.

"A few things, but not much about the Letiche," I say.

"Well, the Letiche is a mysterious creature. You might find some answers by speaking to some locals. I wish you the best of luck."

"Thanks," I say, and Connor takes my backpack, carrying it for me as we leave the classroom. A true gentleman.

△△△

I stop at the library on my way home. I have to be quick about my browsing. I don't want Mom to worry about where I've been, but I need to understand my ability to see Penelope a little bit more before I go confronting her. It's the first day of September, but I don't think Noir has gotten the memo. It's still so sticky out. The air conditioning that blasts on me as soon as I open the library doors is welcoming.

There's no Donna at the front desk. She's busy shelving books. I don't want to bother her, so I decide to find the books I need on my own. Odds are that books about people who can see ghosts will be somewhere in the same section Connor and I were just recently in.

My shoes click loudly across the floor, filling the space with their sound. There aren't too many people milling about today. I would have expected it to be busier here, especially right after school. I guess kids would rather study at home than in the library.

I get to the section of books I need, section three-hundred and ninety. There's a big dent in the books on the shelf from where Connor took some the other day. My hand feels across the spines, scanning the titles. I move further and further down the aisle.

Reaching section one-hundred and thirty, titles about ghosts and the paranormal begin. Finally, the books I want. True ghost stories, haunted houses, and possessions are some of the various categories of books I see on the shelf. I need something a little more psychological.

Then it catches my eye. *The Science of Spirituality*. It doesn't sound super interesting, but the title speaks to me, the words on the spine whispering in my ear that this is the book I need to read.

I place the book on a desk with a loud thud. It's huge! Like a textbook I would have for school. There's no way I'll have time to truly read this before I have to get home, but I figure I can at least thumb through some of it. Looking at the glossary, I turn to the chapter titled "Near Death."

I was touch and go in the hospital for a long time. I'd say I qualify for near death. My eyes soak in the first paragraph, heart beating faster at every word.

It is not uncommon for those experiencing or who have experienced a near-death situation to have some connection or link to the spirit world. Spirits are able to imprint on those who are balancing between the two worlds.

I don't remember much from when I was in the hospital. There were no sounds or visions that I recall. It was all black skies and lullabies. At least, that's what I remember. It's quite possible I'm forgetting something. Maybe my accident really did unlock my ability to see and communicate with Penelope. I wonder if that means I'll be able to see other ghosts.

I look around the library, suddenly self-conscious of someone—or something—watching me. It's completely empty. Nobody around. The clock on the wall says it's almost four. Time for me to leave.

The front desk is empty. There's no sign of Donna, not even where I last saw her shelving books. I ring the bell on the counter, hoping to get Donna's attention. Nothing. I'm trying to fight the rising panic I have in my chest. It's irrational. I know

I'm only feeling like this because of what I've been reading, but I still can't force the feeling away.

The ting of the bell echoes throughout the building as I ring it again. Leaning over the front desk, I look down the dark hallway that leads somewhere into the back of the building. Is the darkness moving?

I hit the bell again, frantic.

I'm tempted to take the book and run, just leave an IOU on the front desk. This is stupid. I scold myself for the fear that's churning in my stomach and march behind the front desk. Donna has to be around here somewhere. The hallway is ominous. A single lightbulb flickering overhead, making the shadows start to crowd around me. There's a door closed ahead of me. Maybe Donna's back there.

My shaky hand reaches for the doorknob...

"What are you doing?"

I scream a blood curdling scream at the sound of her voice behind me. Donna looks just as scared as I am when I quickly turn around. My cheeks are on fire with the amount of embarrassment that burns through them. I'm so glad that nobody else is here to have witnessed this fiasco.

"I am so sorry," I say, hand to my chest trying to slow down my heart rate. "I couldn't find you anywhere. I'm ready to check out now."

Donna turns on her heels toward the front desk, and I follow her with my head hanging the whole way. The epitome of the walk of shame.

"I can see why you're so jumpy," Donna gestures to the book I'm checking out. I give her a tight smile, more than ready to get out of here. Talking to Penelope before knowing she was a ghost was easy, but if this book is enough to give me the creeps, how am I ever going to survive talking to her now?

CHAPTER THIRTEEN

Dad, of course, was on board for fishing the next day. It barely took any convincing. He was so excited about going on one more fishing trip with me before the Fall weather really takes over. Dreary days are ahead of us.

As usual, Linda threw an absolute fit over us going without her.

"You never take me fishing with you!" she wailed.

"That's because you don't even like fishing," I said, which only made her wail more. She stopped whining, though, once Mom promised her they'd do something fun together. Anything to get her to shut up.

Connor met us at the house. I was more than ready to get him out the door before Linda could say anything embarrassing about me. Dressed in an old t-shirt and baseball hat, tacklebox in hand, and fishing pole over his shoulder, Connor looked like a model for a sports magazine. I almost fainted at the sight of him. The ride in Dad's truck to the bayou didn't make things any easier, as Connor's cologne filled my nostrils. I had to keep myself from inhaling deeply like a creep the whole way.

The bayou still makes me uneasy, even in the daytime. No rain in the forecast for today, and the sun shines brightly overhead. It's silly to fear what lurks in the bayou when it's not dark, but I find myself more afraid of being able to see everything around me clearly.

What if there are more ghosts than just Penelope out here?

"Whaddya say we go find a good spot to cast out?" Dad pulls his gear from the truck bed, tucking the lunch cooler Mom packed underneath his arm. I hope she packed some of her peach iced tea. We're going to need it if the day grows any more humid.

We follow my dad through the trees, heading toward the bayou. "So, when are you going to ditch us?" Connor whispers so my dad won't hear.

"In three...two...one..."

"Be safe." And with my dad's back turned, walking ahead of us, Connor acts like he's going to kiss me. Butterflies swirl around my stomach as my dreams of having a high school romance like Molly Ringwald are about to come true. Connor is making a *move!* And if I don't chill out now, my heart is going to beat right out of my chest and splat onto the ground in front of him. *Be cool.*

I step forward to close the space between us, but the light from the sun hits my pendant just right and practically blinds Connor. He trips on the ground, skinning his knee in the process. Thank goodness it's not bad enough to draw any blood. I tuck the pendant into my shirt, feeling horrified that I ruined our potential first kiss.

"Everything okay back there?" My dad glances back, but Connor is already up from the ground and walking again. Neither of us say anything about what just happened. It's easier to just ignore it than to verbalize how embarrassing it was.

Remembering the real reason why we're out here in the first place, I manage to make my voice work again. "Oh shoot. I left my lure back in the truck. I'll catch up with you guys." I turn to leave.

"We've got plenty of lures in the tacklebox, Jen. Just use one of those," my dad says.

My wide eyes look at Connor, whose face resembles my own. "But—"

"It's her lucky lure." Connor saves the day.

"Exactly. I was just telling Connor about it earlier. I want him to see just how lucky it is." Sweat beads across my forehead and it has nothing to do with the humidity.

"Well don't take too long."

I give my dad and Connor a little wave as they go on their way. I pretend to walk toward the direction of the parked truck in case my dad turns around. When I glance behind me and can barely make out their figures, I change my path, heading deeper into the trees.

I don't bother calling out for Penelope. I don't want to say anything too loudly, afraid that Al could make an appearance.

I know she'll come to me. After all, I'm the only one who seems to be able to see and talk to her. I'd imagine it would get pretty lonely not being able to communicate with anyone. Forced to watch those around you walk by like you don't even exist. Not being able to call out to your loved ones. It sounds so...heartbreaking.

I take in my surroundings. I don't know why I was so nervous about coming here in the daytime. The trees are so beautiful, an ominous beauty, but beautiful nonetheless. Various birds chirp around me, flying in and out of the trees, their colorful feathers vibrant against the leaves. The fresh air floods my lungs, filling them with peace and calm. I take a seat underneath one of the giant cypress trees. The ground is moist but it's coolness seeps through my clothes, providing relief from the humidity.

A little, grey squirrel runs across in front of me, kicking up a few fallen leaves behind it. I smile as it scurries up a tree. My eyes shift to the path on the ground that the squirrel created. Footprints imbedded in the mud reveal themselves from underneath the stirred leaves. Whatever crossed through here had large, webbed feet and...what looks like claws. If I had to guess, I'd say they look similar to an alligator, but that would be impossible. These tracks are at least a foot long, and just as wide. The spacing between them doesn't seem right either.

Crawling to the footprints, I hesitantly reach my hand out, tracing their shape with my fingers. Up ahead, the footprints appear to change from clawed feet to human feet. *Raised by alligators...*

"They say you can get lost out here. That the bayou can swallow you whole if you're not careful."

Startled, I fall onto my butt. Penelope comes out from behind a tree across from me. Her skin is stark white, hair muddy brown, water dripping off her clothes. "And, if I remember correctly, I told you to stay away." She narrows her eyes at me.

I stand up, brushing the earth from my pants. "Correction, you told me the bayou isn't safe anymore."

"You didn't hear the warning in that?"

I bite my lip. Of course I heard the warning. I'm just clearly bad at listening.

"How'd you know my name?" I ask.

"What?" She looks at me, dumbfounded. "I give you a warning, that the bayou is dangerous, and all you care about is how I knew your name?"

There's a part of me that's ashamed of myself for ignoring her, but the part that needs to know more takes over, and I don't retreat from my question.

Finally, Penelope lets out an exasperated sigh. "The others talk… about you."

"Others? There are more of you here?" I look around, searching for any signs of more ghosts.

"They aren't here. It's just me."

"What do they say about me?" I'm suddenly self-conscious about what these other spirits think about me.

"You're the girl who walked between two worlds." The hospital. She's referring to when I was in the hospital.

"I—I don't remember anything."

She smirks. "I don't remember anything either. One day, I was alive and breathing. The next, I was here, dead."

My heart sinks when I hear that Penelope has no memory of what happened to her. The whole point of today was to find out what's happening in the bayou, and hopefully see if there's a way to save CeCe. My hope flies away with the birds in the trees.

Penelope sees the look of disappointment on my face. "Don't," she says.

"Don't what?"

"I know what you're thinking. You think that you'll somehow be able to stop whatever is happening here. You can't. The best thing you can do is stay away and tell your friends the same."

"You said that you don't know what happened to you. How do you know that there's something bad out here?"

Her ghostly gaze pierces right through me. "I've seen its eyes. They're golden discs that match the moon. They lurk in the water and watch you wherever you go. There is something evil in the bayou, and it wants all of us dead." She walks away from me.

"Wait!" When she turns, my heart jumps into my throat. I don't know how I missed it before, but there, partially covered by her mud-soaked hair, are bloody wounds that look too similar. My hand searches underneath my hair, feeling the raised bumps where my skull was sewn shut. Penelope touches her head, fear in her eyes as she realizes we're the same. Only, I'm still alive. Penelope disappears in front of me, leaving me alone and stunned. The creature that attacked me had killed Penelope. I was supposed to be just like her. A ghost in the bayou. For some reason, I survived. I don't know how I'll do it, but I'm going to make sure that it doesn't happen to anybody else again.

FEELIN' PARANORMAL PEACH TEA

What you'll need:

2 bags of either black or green tea

14 cups of water (divided)

½ cup of granulated sugar (adjust amount of sugar on how sweet or unsweet you want your tea)

Tea directions:

In a medium saucepan, bring four cups of water to a boil. Add the tea to the water and brew according to your tea bag's packaging. Pour in remaining ten cups of water, and granulated sugar and stir until completely dissolved. Pour in a glass over ice, and stir in fruit compote (however much you desire).

Fruit Compote:

What you'll need:

2 C frozen fruit (peaches)

¼ sugar

1-2 tbs water

Directions:

Add all ingredients to a saucepan and cook over medium heat, stirring occasionally, until sugar dissolves and fruit starts to soften. Turn heat to low and continue to cook, stirring frequently, until mixture starts to thicken. Remove from heat, cover and let cool.

CHAPTER FOURTEEN

The thoughts in my head are a jumbled mess as I make my way back to my dad and Connor. They're both casting their rods, boots in the water, waiting for the fish to take the bait. Red fish are a popular catch in the bayou this time of year, so I wonder if they've had any luck yet. They're laughing at something Connor said which makes me happy.

The fact that Connor can get along with my dad and vice versa when I'm not around is a very good sign. Unfortunately, as excited as I am to see them having a good time, I can't stick around and fish. It doesn't feel right to do something so... human. Especially after finding out I shouldn't still be a human.

No. No negative thoughts allowed.

It's time to go to work and figure out what's going on. To

figure out what caused the injuries to both Penelope and me.

"Hey guys," I say, sidling next to Connor.

"Nice of you to finally join us. I thought you might have gotten lost out there," Dad chuckles. Connor looks serious.

"No, I just don't really feel all that great. A little sick on my stomach. I might be coming down with something." I hold my stomach, pretending that it's really ailing me. "Dad, would it be okay if Connor walked me home?"

Dad reels his line in. "Oh, it's okay kiddo. We can head out."

"No!" Yikes. That was a little too suspicious. "I mean—I don't want to ruin your fishing. After all, you did take off your afternoon to do it. I'll be fine walking. Really."

Thankfully, my dad believes everything I say. "Alright. You guys leave your gear here. Don't want you to have to lug it all the way home. Tell your mom I'll be home after dinner." He faces the bayou, casting his line back out. His bait makes a plopping sound as it hits the water. "Be careful you two," he says, not even glancing back in our direction as we walk away.

The path home from the bayou is starting to become a familiar one. With no sidewalk by the road leading away from the bayou, we're forced to walk through the tall grass. I'm thankful for my long jeans, boots, and the endless amounts of bug spray I used before we left the house.

Traffic out here is sparse with only the occasional car

passing by. There aren't too many houses out on the bayou, and the ones that are out here are spaced very far apart, the closest neighbor being half a mile away. I wonder which one Al lives in. Or maybe he prefers sleeping in a tree. Most of the houses look like dilapidated shacks. Living on the bayou is nothing like living on a lake. It's not very attractive to many home buyers with all the flooding and gators.

Connor is the first to break the silence. "How did things go with Penelope?"

I let out a shaky breath. "I wish I could say they went better. She doesn't remember anything before she died." I avoid a giant mud puddle.

"Like how you don't remember?"

I wince. I know he doesn't mean it in a bad way, but it still frustrates me that I can't remember anything. Not anything before the accident. Not anything during my stay in the hospital. I desperately wish I could remember when I was asleep, in the coma. Where did I go? What could I have seen? Obviously, according to Penelope, there were others who saw me.

"Did she say who—or what—is in the bayou?"

"Not exactly. Just that it's evil and it has yellow eyes." I swallow. "The strangest part about our conversation...we both have the same scars."

"Scars?" Connor grabs my hand. I stop to look at him, his

hazel eyes filled with concern, and something else I can't quite make out.

I hide my scars underneath my hair pretty well. The teasing and hairspray do a good job of masking. But even with them hidden, I still think of them as a beacon on my head. I always assume everyone else in the world can see them from a mile away. I forget that nobody really knows they're there. Well, no one except my family and me. I part my hair, feeling for the bumps along my scalp as I show Connor the scars. To my relief, he doesn't seem to be grossed out.

"So, you guys faced the same monster?"

"Looks like it."

"Interesting." Connor rubs his chest and hums.

We continue our walk to my house, hand in hand. The clouds that have been covering the sky all day have parted a little, exposing a pink sunset sky underneath. Must be getting close to dinner time.

"So, do you have any ideas?" Connor asks. I'm assuming he means on what is in the bayou. If he had asked me a few days ago, I would have probably said it was a crazed murderer. A man with serial killer instincts who preys on children. Now, after my run in with Penelope the ghost, I wonder if there's something more supernatural out in the bayou.

Images of the footprints in the mud flash through my

mind like crime scene photos. They weren't normal gator prints. It was as if a gator turned into... No. I can't complete that thought. At least not right now. I'm just learning to accept the fact that I've seen and communicated with a ghost. I don't know if I can make my brain wrap anything else around itself at the moment. All I know is that I can't put it off, not if I want to prevent it from happening again.

Instead of answering Connor, I just shake my head. Even though I know he'd be encouraging about any of my theories, I need to figure things out for myself first.

"Maybe it's just because I've been pretty invested in Mr. C's class, but I can't help but think that maybe it could be Big Foot out there wreaking havoc in the bayou."

I stiffen at his remark. He has no idea that I'm having similar thoughts roaming around in my own head. Connor takes my cue of silence and squeezes my hand. The sound of the wind is the only thing that can be heard the rest of the way home.

△△△

I don't run up the stairs to my room until I hear Connor's car backing down the driveway, which isn't difficult to hear. It's so loud that it rattles the windows. I think the muffler must have fallen off at some point.

I shut the door and my nerves quickly go from ones of anxiousness to annoyance when I see Linda laying on her stomach across my bed flipping through one of my teen magazines. "I'm sorry, I forgot when this became your room," I throw my boots into my closet.

She continues to flip through the magazine, feet up in the air behind her. If she wasn't such a brat, I'd think she was a cute kid. With her yellow dress on, and icy hair in pigtails, she looks so young and innocent. "Do you hope Connor kisses you like Brand kisses Andy in *The Goonies*?"

Ugh! She's such a creep! I rip the magazine from her hands, tearing the Whitney Houston cover in the process. "Get out of my room!" I seethe, hitting her with the magazine. The little worm runs out of my room, slamming the door shut and giggling down the hall. Sometimes—most times—she really makes my blood boil.

My body is hot after dealing with Linda. Partially because of anger, but even I must admit to myself that a lot of it is because of embarrassment. I grab my pillow, pulling it to my face, and scream. Much better.

The books from the library stare back at me from across the room, their words begging to be read, beckoning me to crack open their spines. I hear their pages like a siren's call. Time to get to work.

I start my bookworm journey through the pages of the book on spirits, where I learn that certain ghosts and humans can be tethered through experiences.

Stories have been told for centuries of people receiving warnings or visions from spirits trying to keep them safe. Most often these warnings and visions are based off a spirit's own personal experience. For example, a person about to board a plane may receive a vision from a spirit who died on a plane, telling them not to go.

I can see and speak to Penelope, but to my knowledge, I haven't been able to see or speak to any other ghosts. It's possible that the reason I can see Penelope is because we both were attacked by the same... monster.

As much as I'd love to read more of this book, *Shapeshifted* glares at me from across the room like a jealous girlfriend. I need to study for my essay. Sprawling out onto my bed, I turn to the last place I left off. The Letiche.

People have been going missing for decades throughout the Southern states, the states where the Letiche can blend in the most amongst the gators. There are so many sketches of different creatures on the pages. One is labelled "Letiche" underneath. It's the image of a monster with the face of a gator and the body of a man, towering over a victim. Another picture shows a gator creature the size of a giant wrestler, muscles bulging from its body, walking around on two feet.

Like the footprints.

Could it be possible that the Letiche is lurking somewhere in Noir? Walking around like a human one minute, and a monster the next?

I'm suddenly aware of how quiet it is in the house. The silence makes me feel paranoid. I close the book, not wanting to look at the Letiche anymore. I put my Phil Collins vinyl on. His voice drowns out the eerie hush and I welcome it.

Instead of picking the book back up from where I left off, I turn to the section that discusses the characteristics of a shapeshifter. Mr. C discussed it a little in his class before but didn't go into the amount of detail that this book does.

While some shapeshifters are free to transform into any form, most shapeshifters are limited to their transformations. For example, a shapeshifter with the lycanthrope gene will only be able to transform into canine creatures, i.e. a werewolf.

I would assume that the Letiche has some form of gene that makes it limited to transforming between alligator and human. Maybe I'll include that theory in my essay.

There are shapeshifters that are able to shift at will, whereas others are limited to when they can.

I wonder which category the Letiche lands in for when it can or can't shift.

I want to read more, but my stomach rumbles, reminding me that I forgot to eat dinner. Its demand for food is only getting louder.

What kind of food does the Letiche eat?

I shake the thought from my mind, not wanting to lose my appetite.

The stairs creak under my feet as I make my way down to the kitchen. Sure enough, I was so invested in reading that I completely missed dinner. Thank goodness for leftovers. The fridge is full of them, and I happily pull out the container marked "fried okra." Yum.

Linda is sitting on the living-room floor, watching an episode of *Scooby Doo*. Of course. I don't mind, though, I really like this show. This episode is a good one. I find myself invested with the mystery as I pop fried okra in my mouth. A werewolf in a funny, green suit howls at the full moon, getting ready to chase Scooby and Shaggy. The episode ends, and the next one begins.

"I want some of that," Linda says, reaching for the container in my lap, to which I slap her little grubby hand away.

"You already ate dinner." I turn the TV up louder to block out her protests. The monster pops up on the screen, and my fried okra suddenly turns sour. Gator Ghoul. The alligator beast that is trying to scare the gang. A cartoon gator that makes me feel cold all over. I touch my scars. I wonder if Gator Ghoul isn't so fictional after all.

CHAPTER FIFTEEN

It's a weird experience to have people in your life that you really care about. Not that I don't care about my family, even when Linda gets under my skin, but there were so many months where my only "friends" were the doctors and nurses that I've constantly been in touch with. They're all really nice, but they've obviously never been true friends. They've just been the people who have been there for me. People who have had my back while I've gone through a hard transition.

The nurses have always done their best to make me feel like a normal kid as they do whatever tests it is they need to do. They joke around with me, never talk down to me, and try to relate to me on any level they can. It makes me feel good, but I've always known it's because it's their job.

Now I know what it's like to have true friends, people that

truly care about me and want to be there for me, and it's not because it's their job. Which is why I feel so scared when my alarm goes off for school today. My stomach is all knotted in nerves as my thoughts wander. Am I going to show up today to find that another one of my friends has gone missing?

There's no fancy breakfast spread on the table this morning. It's not a special occasion today, so Mom has decided to keep breakfast simple. Cereal, and to my relief, blueberry muffins. The carton of milk sits on the counter, liquid drops scattered across the surface from Linda's poor attempt at pouring it herself. Picking up the carton to clean up the mess, my heart sticks in my throat.

CeCe's black and white face looks up at me. My eyes tear up and blur her beautiful features. Seeing Penelope's face on the milk carton wasn't easy because I knew she was my age, but I know CeCe—or at least I *knew* her. I suck in a sob.

CeCe blinks.

No. That's not possible. I rub my eyes to clear the tears away.

CeCe narrows her eyes at me. "You need to stop the cycle. The bayou isn't safe, but you have the tool to stop it from—" I don't hear the rest of her sentence as the carton slips from my hand and crashes to the floor, milk exploding in every direction.

"Jensen!" Mom comes bursting into the kitchen. She

instantly drops to the floor with the kitchen rag in her hand. "Look at this mess. I guess I'll be going to the store for more milk today," she huffs. I'm stunned, my now empty hand still shaking in midair. "Don't just stand there. Get the mop." Her words aren't registering. The ringing in my ears is overpowering anything she could possibly be saying to me right now. CeCe's voice is imprinted inside of me, blocking out all other noise.

Seeing ghosts in the bayou is one thing. Seeing talking images on a carton of milk is a whole other thing.

My skin feels clammy and I wonder if my face is as pale as the milk splattered on the floor. It must be because Mom has forgotten the mess and can't stop looking up at me. "Jensen, sweetheart." She pushes off the floor, bringing a hand to my forehead. "You feel feverish. Honey, are you okay?" I can see the look of concern cross over her features, her eyebrows furrowed with worry. I wish I could say something. She steers me to the kitchen table, carefully sitting me down in a chair. "I'm calling the doctor."

I want to protest. I can feel my insides screaming at me to tell her "no," but my body just feels limp, like I'm a puppet waiting for someone else to make me come to life. So, instead of telling my mom that I feel fine, I watch her flit out of the kitchen and take the phone off the hook. Maybe the doctor will tell me this is all just some crazy after effect of the coma. They might just say that I've conjured up the missing kids, ghosts, and monsters in my mind. That none of it exists and I can go back to living my life horror story free. Then again, I don't think they make a pill for any of this.

ΔΔΔ

The light blinds me, leaving my eyes watering. The smell of sterilizing chemicals permeates the air, burning my nose hair. I feel a sneeze coming on. Paper crinkles beneath me as I adjust my position.

The doctor's office will never be my favorite place. Nothing against the people that work here, but this place is like purgatory for me. There is always a fear of being admitted again, that the doctor is going to find something wrong with me and they'll need to run more tests. I just don't want to be trapped here. I spent too many years trapped here already. I spent too many days here after I woke up. Too many months of therapy before I was cleared, only having to come in for the occasional check-up.

That's what I keep reminding myself of now. Today is just a regular check-up because I freaked my mom out.

Dr. Saunders, glasses on the tip of her nose and chestnut hair pulled into a bun, jots down some notes on the clipboard in her well-manicured hands. My fingers fidget in my lap at the possibilities of what she could be writing. My mom sits in the chair next to the door, her leg bouncing up and down as she waits for the results of my exam.

Setting the clipboard on the counter against the wall, Dr. Saunders faces us both. "Well, Mrs. Swells."

"Catie," my mom interrupts her.

"Oh, yes, Catie," she continues. "Everything seems to be checking out great. No changes to the pupils, her speech is fine, scars look great." She leans against the counter. "In a lot of cases, after a head injury such as Jensen's, there can be long term side effects."

"Yes, we're aware of that. It's just that this is the first time anything out of the normal has happened. It's been almost ten months. I think I just assumed we were in the clear."

"These things don't always pop up overnight. Sometimes it can take years for side effects to show."

I wish I could tell them both that the only side effect I'm suffering from is seeing dead people, but I imagine that would end up with me sitting in a psychiatric ward. So, I don't say anything as Dr. Saunders explains what I can do to help prevent the side effects, her voice sounding far away as my ears tune her out.

The car ride home is quiet. Mom keeps watching me from

her peripheral. I don't think she believes the doctor. She probably thinks I could break at any minute.

"I'm fine, Mom," I say, catching her gaze.

She puts her eyes back onto the road, making the turn into our driveway. "I know, I know," she says, trying to pretend she hasn't been monitoring me the whole time. "But..." There's the 'but' again. "Maybe all this has been too much. We should have eased things back in slowly." She puts the car in park.

"Eased what in slowly?"

"School, activities. What would you think about going to classes two days a week and then maybe later on we can work in a full week of school?"

"No!" I shout it loud, but it seems even louder in the confined space of the car. "I haven't known what normal is for a really long time and now you want to take the one thing that makes me feel normal away?" Tears threaten to burst from my eyes.

Mom reaches across the seat, pulling me into a hug. "Shhh," she tries to soothe. "I'm just saying it might be an option, okay? If these spells keep happening. We have to think of your health." She pulls back and looks into my eyes, wiping away a tear that's escaped.

"These spells" meaning my ability to see ghosts. Her believing that my freak out moment earlier was a medical problem and not just because I saw our milk carton talking is potentially going to take away my freedom. I can't lose what I just got back. Trying to keep that freedom may mean that I have to give up on Penelope and CeCe, and leave the mystery of the bayou in the bayou.

CHAPTER SIXTEEN

Today is not going to go well. I can already tell by the amount of looks I'm getting that I'm going to be the center of attention for the rest of the day. Whispers about where the coma girl was yesterday are probably swirling around, which is moste likely the reason for all the stares. Even with all eyes on me, that's not what has me feeling jittery. Moira and Connor are standing guard at my locker, their eyes both widening in surprise at my appearance.

Moira is ready to pounce while Connor looks like he's going to shield me from everything Moira wants to verbally throw at me.

"Where were you yesterday? We thought you were one of them, Jen." Moira is talking a mile a minute.

"One of who, Moira?" I ask nonchalantly, side-stepping her

to get to my locker.

She scoffs. "One of the missing kids, duh."

I knew what she meant, but I'm trying to act like I don't care. I can't care. After the conversation with my mom yesterday, I came to the realization that the missing kids are not my responsibility. Penelope and CeCe are not my responsibility. They can't be.

My locker sticks and Connor steps up to open it for me, but I block his path and use his locker trick myself. The locker pops open. Connor looks a little hurt that I didn't let him help me. I don't know why I'm acting like this. The whole reason I've decided to not insert myself in the bayou mystery is because I want to continue to be able to come to school. I want to be able to be with my friends, but right now I just feel numb.

"Earth to Jensen," Moira waves her hands in front of my face. "What's your problem? Is it Penelope?"

I shut the locker, moving past them. "It's nothing."

They flank me on either side, Moira looking to Connor with a worried expression. "Connor told me what happened with Penelope the other day. Is there something else you aren't telling us? We can go to the bayou this weekend to check things —"

"No, Moira." I stop walking and take a deep breath. "No more bayou. No more Penelope. No more monsters," my voice shakes. It's taking everything in me to speak these words, but it has to be done.

Moira looks taken aback. Her mouth opens and closes like she doesn't know how to respond.

Connor is the first to speak up. "I thought you wanted to stop what's happening out there?"

I do. I want to stop it so badly. I want to track down the monster that stole four years of my life and make it pay, but at what cost?

"If something was taken from you, something so important, and you just got it back, would you take a risk that could potentially take it away again?" Silence follows my question. "Exactly. Neither of you would. This isn't *Scooby Doo*. We don't unmask villains. We're teenagers that live in reality and we need to start acting like it."

Moira gapes at me like I'm a stranger, like she can't believe it was me who said all that. Her eyes narrow as she crosses her arms over her chest. She looks like she wishes she could breathe fire in my direction. I steel myself against the words I know she's about to spew.

"You're right. This isn't some cartoon. This is real life, and in real life people are dying. Not just people, though, teenagers who are just like us. Teenagers who are just like you." I flinch as she continues. "Those scars on your head, the ones Connor told me about, those are your battle scars. You came out on top for a reason and I can only imagine that it's because you're meant to put an end to all of this. You're meant to help Penelope find peace."

Tears are threatening to spill from her eyes, but I can tell she isn't going to let them fall. "So, yeah, you can be scared, Jensen. That's normal. Kind of like the normal you've been craving. But what isn't normal is turning your back on people who need you. As for me, I'm going to do the best I can to keep my friends safe, with or without you." Moira spins, braids whipping behind her as she stomps away, anger dripping off her and spilling into the air around her as everyone looks at me with sour expressions for offending the Queen B.

Connor's looking down at his Converse, not wanting to meet my gaze.

"Connor, you have to understand—"

He holds up his hand, stopping my sentence. "You don't need to explain anything to me, Jensen. I understand. Besides, we're just teenagers. What can we honestly do to help? I think you're making the right decision."

Connor's reaction makes me feel a little bit better, but it hurts to know that he's the only friend I have right now. I thought by turning away from all the stuff going on in the bayou I'd be saving my friendships. I thought it was the only way to continue to live my life like a normal teenager. But I was wrong. Everything I was afraid of happening has happened. One of the people I've grown closest to in the last few weeks has just walked away from me, and I don't know if I'll be able to get her back.

△△△

The brown, paper lunch bag feels heavy in my hand as I make my way through the cafeteria. All eyes are on me, they have been all week since my argument with Moira in the hallway. I thought that we would be able to move past all of this within a day, but it's been three since we last spoke. Lunch was the one place where I thought we would eventually clear the air and move on. Those hopes have been shattered and my heart sinks deeper every day whenever I see my table of friends dispersed at different tables.

Moira sits with a group of girls I recognize but don't know. She glares at me as I walk past, the rest of her table following her lead, and I shrink back under their gazes. It's all true. You really don't want to get on Queen B's bad side.

At a circular table across the room, Mabel sits with Mark. They're too caught up in their conversation to pay me any attention, but I already know that after Mabel's blow up the other day, I won't be welcomed at their table, so I keep walking.

Valerie weaves down the aisle to my left. She doesn't seem to have a clear path, so I shift in her direction, hoping that she'll want to sit with me. She doesn't even make eye contact. Instead, she brushes right past me, bumping my shoulder in the process, acting like I don't even exist. Plopping her tray down, she straightens her bright blue dress and sits next to Mabel, jumping right into their conversation.

Greg is nowhere to be found, probably spending some extra time on the football field. And of course, no CeCe. If only Connor shared our lunch period. Then I'd at least have someone to talk to.

I take a seat at my lonely table in the back of the room. It's the most neglected table in the cafeteria. Not even the light above my head works. A shadowed, little alcove forgotten by everyone except the dust bunnies that litter the floor at my feet. The janitors must know that nobody ever chooses to sit here, so why bother with tidying it up.

From my nook, I get a clear view of the whole room. Everyone is sitting with their friends laughing and chatting about whatever, and I can see it now. Without my group of friends sitting in the middle of the room at our usual table, this place has turned into every high-school I've ever seen in movies. And I'm the one who's to blame.

I suddenly think that my mom's threat of school only a

few times a week is a better alternative.

My peanut butter sandwich is like sand in my mouth. My stomach rumbles, but there's no way I can swallow it without wanting to throw it back up. I spit the chewed bite into my paper bag, tossing the rest of the sandwich in after it.

The bell rings and everyone passes by me in a blur, all heading to their next classes, but I'm not ready to follow suit. Curling up on the bench, I lie down and close my eyes. Being alone isn't so bad when you're asleep. It's being awake and alone that feels suffocating. As I drift off to sleep, I hope that when I wake up things will be back to normal, that all my friends will want to be my friends again. *It was all just a bad dream.*

Except when the lunch lady nudges me out of my nap, her disposable gloves still on her hands, I remember nothing has changed. Reality sets in and it's time for me to face it.

CHAPTER SEVENTEEN

Going to school is the worst. Things are even more terrible than they were before.

I tried talking to Moira a couple days ago. She slammed her locker in my face. I won't even try to get Mabel or Valerie's attention. I'm afraid of what they'll do.

Keeping my head down and minding my business is the only way I'm managing to get through these days. Connor has been helping me with my essay, but he gets uncomfortable any time we research the bayou.

Mom and Dad have stopped asking me how my day was. Even Linda has taken the hint and has done her best to not get under my skin the last week.

Every day is like clockwork, now. Wake up. Eat. School. Home. Eat. Homework. Sleep. Repeat.

Nothing exciting.

No hanging out with my friends.

No adventures in the bayou.

No ghosts.

Pushing Penelope out of my mind has been the hardest thing. I keep having nightmares about her. She comes to me, out of the darkness of the bayou, hair dripping wet, and the full moon lit brightly behind her, and she says it's hunting us. And then, without fail, sharp teeth clamp around my ankles, and I wake up. Every. Single. Night. Always the same nightmare, always waking up at the same time.

"Jen, time for dinner!' Mom calls up the stairs. I'm not hungry. I don't feel like moving from my bed. Even my voice is too tired to respond. So, I don't. My mom already knows I'm going through some things at school, so she doesn't push, though I know she wants to.

The bed and all my pillows are too comfortable to abandon. I wonder if this is what depression feels like, never wanting to leave your bed, not even for food.

I start to drift off to sleep, but when I hear Penelope's soft voice reach out, I force my eyes open. There will be none of that right now. I don't want to think about the ghost girl. A heavy sigh pushes out between my lips.

Logically, I know the only way to stop the nightmares, to

never see Penelope in my dreams again, is to go back into the bayou.

The piece of paper from the book is still where I put it a week ago. In my trash can. I crumpled it up and tossed it in an attempt to move on. A silent whisper crosses the room from where it's discarded, beckoning me to pick it up and memorize its words once again.

I do just that. Tearing myself away from the tangled bed sheets, I take the paper from the pink bin. The words haven't changed at all but, rereading the page along with the notes I added before, clearer thoughts start to piece themselves together.

In the werewolf mythology, the transformation from man to werewolf requires the light of a full moon. It's clear from the book that the Letiche is believed to be a shapeshifting creature, and the legend sounds very similar to that of a werewolf. Which means the Letiche must use the full moon in order to transform. And just like a werewolf is a man by day…

The hair on my neck tingles.

The Letiche is doubling as a man—or woman—hiding amongst the rest of society. What if that person is in Noir right now? What if the Letiche isn't merely a legend, but a true story? From the scrap of paper left in the book, I believe someone else had these same questions.

I jot down everything I've learned in the past few weeks from the books I've read, Penelope, and the things that Connor has told me.

Connor's eyes flash in my mind, the perfect hazel shade. His dimple that's like magic when it appears. His voice echoes in my head, laughing with me, calling me "Jen." And then his voice mentions that the Letiche hides along the Southern states.

Is it possible that the Letiche changes its location every few years to blend in better? Or maybe so it doesn't get caught?

I decide to thumb through the pages of the book. I want to see if cryptids have some type of migration pattern, which sounds absolutely ridiculous, but in my head, it makes the most sense.

The front cover falls open, revealing the stamped list of checkouts. Names that don't have any meaning date all the way back to the thirties. It's the very last checkout date and name that makes my eyes feel like they're going to bug out of my head.

Albert Fortner.

The stench of putrid body odor fills my nostrils as the ghostly pressure of invisible arms wraps around my belly. I throw the book out of my hands and onto the floor like it could burn me at any second.

Albert Fortner. Al. The man from the bayou. The one that Moira said her Mammy had known. There's a chance that Moira's

Mammy and Al may know more about what's going on in the bayou than anybody else.

It's like I have the puzzle pieces all laid out in front of me and they're slowly starting to come together. I just need a few more pieces to help me get the full picture. And I think those pieces are going to require me to seek Moira's help.

I run my hands through my hair. I'm going to need all the courage I can muster to confront her. Time to put on my big girl pants and apologize.

∆∆∆

I couldn't find Moira anywhere before school started. She wasn't at any of her usual hangouts around the building. Nausea had settled into my belly just thinking about where she could have possibly been, and if she was even here.

Relief sweeps over me, though, when I walk into lunch and see her sitting with her new table of friends. Her dark braids are perfectly plaited into one giant braid that rests against her back. And, in pure Moira fashion, her outfit looks like it was plucked straight from the pages of a magazine. Her acid wash, denim jumpsuit, and jade green, plaid button up underneath is to die for.

My sneakers squeak across the floor, the September rain

making it impossible to stay dry, as I make my way to her table. I have to keep readjusting the grip on the book as my hands grow even more moist with anxious sweat the closer I get. She hasn't spotted me yet, which makes me feel more confident. As long as her gaze doesn't meet mine before I reach her, there will be no chance I chicken out.

Why does this make me more nervous than talking to a ghost?

I come up from behind Moira and slam the book open in front of her. Okay, so not exactly the most subtle way to go about this, but it gets her attention.

She jumps back on the bench and places her hand against her chest. "What the heck, Jensen?"

I clearly scared her. And judging from the looks of everyone else at the table, they think I'm crazed too. Maybe I should have started with the apology?

I try to muster out the words, "I'm sorry," but they're caught in my throat, wrapped around my tongue. I guess my big girl pants don't fit very well, because all I can think about is how I deserve an apology, too.

I point to Albert's name on the page. "What does your Mammy know about Albert Fortner?"

Moira glances around at all her new friends, acting like she has no idea who the weird girl is asking her about her Mammy.

"What are you talking about?" she scoffs. Okay, so she wants to play the hard way.

"You said your Mammy knew Al. You told me that he wasn't behind what's happening in the bayou, yet here his name is in my book." I see that Valerie, Mabel, Mark, and Greg are all eyeing us from their table across the room.

Moira smiles, a fake smile. I know because I've made the same face before. "Excuse us one moment," she gets up from the table and grips my arm. I quickly snag the book from the table as she drags me across the room, down the hall, and into the girl's bathroom.

I'm not sure I've been in this bathroom before, but it looks like all the others in the school. The green tile on the floors matches the green of the lockers in the hallways. Beige paint coats the walls, while three sinks with dirty mirrors above them are lined up to the left. To the right are three stalls, one handicapped, with green doors. The light fixtures are fluorescent bulbs that make anyone look like they've come down with a cold.

Floral scented soap mixed with pee and cigarettes is the aroma that drifts through the air, gagging me as we step through the swinging door. The single window against the far wall is open, but it doesn't help the smell. This bathroom must not get much attention, which explains the cigarette smoke wafting through the air and out the window. Easier not to get caught in here.

Moira marches over to the last stall, and with a strength I didn't know she had, she blasts through it. Sitting on the toilet, cigarette in hand, is a girl I recognize from my English class. Heather, I think, is her name.

"Out," Moira demands. Heather is about to protest, but then she sees who's making the demands and quickly flushes her cigarette and rushes out of the bathroom. Moira stomps to the door and turns the lock, then she whips her head around to face me. "Care to explain why you all of a sudden want to play detective now? Because last I checked, you wanted no part of it." She crosses her arms over her chest.

I throw my hands up, hypothetically waving my white flag. "I get it. I deserved the cold shoulder. I just—I was afraid my mom would pull me from school if I kept digging into things. But not talking to you these past few weeks has been torture. I'd rather be homeschooled."

Moira's shoulders sag. "It just felt like you were abandoning ship…abandoning Penelope and CeCe. And since none of the rest of us can communicate with them, it made me mad." Moira places a hand on my shoulder. "I might have overreacted a bit. Sometimes my Queen B flares up."

I smile. "I think we all overreacted. Sorry?"

"Sorry," she holds her hand out and I shake it. "Now, what exactly were you saying about my Mammy?" Someone bangs on the door. "Occupied!" Moira shouts.

"I really have to goooo!" someone cries on the other side.

Moira makes a loud dry heaving sound. "Sorry, but you're not going to want to be in here." She heaves again, and I hold a hand over my mouth to suppress my laughter.

"Oh gross!" the person outside the door yells in disgust, then we hear footsteps retreating away from the door.

I fist bump Moira. "Nice heaving work. Very believable."

"Thank you, thank you," Moira bows. "Now, spill. What about Mammy?"

We both take a seat on the counter that holds the sinks. "You said your Mammy knew Al, the guy from the bayou, right?"

"Yeah. She knew him from high school. She said he's always been a strange guy, sort of a loner, but that he's completely harmless."

"Well, I've been doing a lot of research for Mr. C's class."

"The one about the mythological creatures?" she interrupts, and I nod my head. "Connor won't shut up about that class."

I smile. I know how much he loves that class, and he's been even more focused on it since he's been helping me with my essay.

"In my research for this essay, I've been studying a lot about shapeshifter legends. The main topic I've been focusing on is about a creature called Letiche." I wait to see if there's any reaction from her, like maybe she's heard of it before, but her vacant stare tells me that she has no idea what I'm talking about. "The Letiche moves from swampland to swampland across the Southern States. And—hear me out—I think it's the reason behind the missing kids." Moira blinks at me.

"And the Letiche is what exactly?" Moira frowns.

"A shapeshifting alligator person. The legend says it was a child born of the Devil and raised by alligators. Whatever being born of the Devil means. And I think the moonlight is what triggers the shift." I take a breath, biting my lip at what I'm about to say next. "Not just any moonlight, though. A full moon. Like a werewolf."

Moira raises her eyebrows, and I can't tell if she thinks I'm joking or if she actually believes me. My stomach clenches as she shifts her legs, crossing them over each other, trying to decide what she's going to say next. "And you have proof of this? Or is Mr. C just getting to your head?"

Dang it. Of course, she would ask for proof.

"I don't have exact proof; just clues I've been piecing together. There were some footprints—too large for a normal gator—in the bayou, and next to those were human footprints.

I noticed them when I went to talk to Penelope. And Penelope and I have matching scars. I mean, mine are scars, hers were still open wounds. She also mentioned something about yellow eyes in the water." There's the distant sound of the bell ringing, but neither of us react to it. What's one tardy slip if it means we're going to potentially save lives?

"So, you and Penelope have a spiritual connection because the same monster attacked you?" Moira leans forward, eager to hear more.

I nod my head in response. "I'm pretty sure that's why. I saw CeCe too. Her picture talked to me from a milk carton." And if Moira didn't think I was ridiculous before, she must now.

"Is CeCe okay? Did she tell you anything important?" Moira grabs my wrist in a tight hold. I guess I still seem pretty sane.

"I dropped the milk before I could even comprehend what she was saying."

"Oh." Moira looks sullen. "So, what does my Mammy and Al have to do with any of this?"

I rub my hands together, suddenly feeling cold. "I think your Mammy might be wrong about Al." I open the cover of *Shapeshifted* to where the list of previous checkouts is, and I hand it and the note to Moira. Pointing to the page, I direct her eyes to the name that had caught my attention. "Is Albert

Fortner the same Al your Mammy knows?"

Moira doesn't take her eyes off the book. "It's possible," she skims the pages.

"I'm pretty sure Albert Fortner wrote the note. He was the last one to check the book out, so it makes sense to me that he would have been the one to leave the note behind."

"I think the best way for us to try and solve this mystery would be to talk to my Mammy ourselves."

CHAPTER EIGHTEEN

Mammy's house happens to be in the Old District of Noir. My dad drives us here every so often as a way to get us out of the house. He likes to tell us about the history of Noir and how it all starts with the Old District.

The Old District is home to battle grounds from the Civil War. These spots are marked by memorials, statues, and small museums. Occasionally, you'll pass a smaller colonial house that has some type of war story. Then there are the plantation houses that are filled with sordid stories. The history behind each structure seems to ooze from their very shingles.

The soil is rich with blood of lives lost and the air is filled with the spirits left behind. It's the reason I don't like coming to the Old District. It gives me the heebie jeebies.

Most of the houses are large in stature, with columns

that make them look proud, and are guarded by wrought iron gates. Weeping willows and cypress trees shade the houses from the harsh light, and protect them from nasty weather. White, pristine paint makes them stand out amongst all the greenery and the dull, gray sky. While most yards in Louisiana are overgrown jungles due to the humidity, the yards in the Old District are perfectly manicured.

Moira's mom, Claire, pulls into the circular driveway, the car lurching down the gravel path. Moira looks just like her mom. Their hair is both done the same way and their clothing style is very similar. They clearly know what's hot in the eighties. If I hadn't already been introduced to her mom, I would have assumed they were sisters.

"Looks like Mam decided to leave the porch light on for us." Claire turns the engine off.

Sure enough, the porch light is on, leaving a ghostly glow in the evening fog. As we walk the little pathway to the front, Mammy's house comes into full view. The place is huge. It's the type of house that would require a map so you don't get lost. There's a wraparound porch with some wicker patio chairs resting in the corner, a tea table in between them. Slowly, I make my way up the steps behind Moira and Claire, completely in awe of the home we're about to enter. The front door is daunting with its old, lion shaped knockers. Moira reaches her hand up to knock, but the door eerily creaks open before she touches the knocker.

"Cher, you know you never have to knock here." A beautiful woman stands on the other side of the door. Her dark skin is rich against the glow of the porch lamp, her brown eyes standing out against her gold eyeshadow. Her hair is tied back, braided, and beaded with the most unique accessories. Red framed glasses, that match her ruby lipstick, rest on the edge of her nose. Her blue slacks and white button-up seem casual, but the silk ascot wrapped around her neck shows her class. Chunky bangles adorn her arms while gold hoops dangle from her ears. This must be Mammy.

Moira and Claire wrap their arms around Mammy. "Mam, this is my friend, Jensen," Moira looks up at Mammy and waves an arm in my direction.

Mammy shuffles toward me and pulls me into a hug. "It's so good to meet you, cher. I've heard so much about you."

She has? I raise an eyebrow in Moira's direction. She shrugs her shoulders and mouths "not me," which confuses me at first, but then I remember Moira mentioning that Mammy is sensitive to things. Does this mean that Mammy could have heard about me from...the spirit world?

"Don't worry, your secret is safe with me," Mammy whispers in my ear then pulls away with a wink. "Claire, why don't you help me in the kitchen. Gumbo is on the stove. Girls, if you could busy yourselves by setting the table."

I follow Moira down a long hallway, our shoes echoing across the floor. "Should I have taken my shoes off?" I ask, as I think about all the dirt I could be leaving on the polished, hardwood floors.

Moira just shakes her head. "It's fine. Mam has a housekeeper. Not that there is ever anything for the housekeeper to do. Mam enjoys cleaning things." I knew it. Moira's family is rich. As if the whole housekeeper thing isn't enough to clue me in on their wealth, the chandelier that hangs from the dining room ceiling is a definite indication. It is gorgeous, extravagant, and I feel like I have been swept back in time. This is the type of chandelier that you see in movies when the characters go to some ornate ball.

The table in the center of the room is a large, oak table, big enough to seat at least fourteen people. "Does your Mammy use this room often?"

Moira snorts. "Only for special occasions. Consider yourself the guest of honor." Well, that makes me feel nervous.

With the table set, only using the finest china and silverware made with real silver, Mammy and Claire step into the room with a steaming pot of gumbo that they set in the center of the table. It seems a bit silly to sit at this table when it's only the four of us, but it does make me feel like I'm some type of royalty.

Taking the ladle from the pot, I scoop some gumbo up and slosh it into my fancy bowl. The spices from the gumbo reach up and tickle my nose, causing me to sneeze. "Hope you don't mind a little kick in your gumbo," Mammy says, nodding in my direction. I shake my head. I don't want to be rude, but spicy food and I don't really get along. I just hope I don't choke on the gumbo. That would be tragic.

To my relief, the spice isn't strong enough to send me into a coughing fit. It is absolutely delicious. "The gumbo is fantastic," I say through mouthfuls.

"I'm glad you like it," Mammy replies. "Now, Mo said you had some questions you wanted to ask me. I'm all ears." The gumbo squirms in my belly. I shift my eyes from Moira to Claire, not entirely sure I want Moira's mom to hear everything. "Don't worry, cher, Claire here is just as understandin' as the rest of us. Nothin' is too strange in our world."

"In your world?"

"The supernatural has always been a part of this family. We've shared a deep connection with it since way back, before I was even born. It's the Lafayette family legacy."

"My questions are less supernatural and more investigative." Mammy motions for me to go on. I push my bowl of gumbo away. I won't be able to finish it. "What do you know about Albert Fortner?"

Mammy sets her spoon down and wipes her mouth with a cloth napkin. "Albert Fortner—Al—was someone I knew in high school. Later on, after we'd graduated and I had children of my own, Al went a little off the deep end." She clasps her hands together. "It was the sixties, a time when crime was low, and kids stayed out all hours. The front doors were left unlocked. Anyone was welcome. Until kids started goin' missin'."

"Like now," Moira interrupts.

Mammy shakes her head. "Like now. Old Al worked for the police force at one time. He swore up and down that he knew what was doin' it. Went on and on about how the gator in the swamp was snatching the boys and girls up, eatin' their bodies and feastin' on their souls. He spent every day in that swamp lookin' for the supposed creature, until eventually he decided to live out there. Left his job and everythin'. He moved into this tiny little shack on the edge of the bayou. Everyone thought he'd lost his mind." She audibly gulps, a look of guilt crossing her features. "Myself included. I tried to talk sense into the man. I warned him about the authorities thinkin' he'd taken those kids, but he wouldn't listen. 'The Letiche got them,' he'd said. And at the time I had no idea what he meant."

I swallow. "Do you know what that means now?"

"I went to my own mother to ask her what Al could

possibly be ramblin' on about. When I tell you I saw the blood drain right out of her face, I mean it. She looked like she could have fainted. 'It's back' was all she could say."

"How long has this been going on? Missing kids in the bayou?" I ask. If Mammy's mother knew about the Letiche, then I'd have to assume it's been a long time.

"As long as the Lafayette's have been in Noir, and that's a very long time." She leans closer across the large table. "You see, the Letiche is a curse on this land. The Lafayette's tried banishin' it long ago, but dark magic is much stronger than anythin' my family could use to combat it."

"Where did the curse come from?" Moira has gumbo dripping from her chin, completely engrossed in the story, and not caring to wipe it off.

"Years ago, when the war was ragin' and there was no peace, the natives begged the soldiers to leave the land alone. It was sacred to them. But their pleas went unheard, and so, they conjured a curse. Anyone who disrupted the Southern lands would only have havoc brought upon them and their children. Nature would come back to seek its revenge. And this revenge came in the form of the Letiche. Born of the Devil—"

"Raised by gators," I finish the tale. "Were the natives spared from the curse?"

Mammy shakes her head. "For a time. The natives had a

way to control the beast. A sacred trinket that would protect them and allow them to have power over the Letiche's life. But, like so many other things that get lost over time, the trinket was lost, and the natives no longer had control over the monster they conjured."

"Why has no one tried to kill it?" I twist in my chair, feeling uncomfortable because of this story.

Mammy laughs which startles all of us. "Child, do you honestly think anyone believes in curses anymore?" Silence follows her question. "Exactly. It's the reason why Al was shunned and labelled a wild man. It's easier for everyone to believe that it's a human committin' these acts."

"Then why haven't you tried to do anything about it?" I ask, accusation rising in my voice. She's known about it all along, she should at least try something.

Anger flashes in her eyes, but she sucks in a shaky breath to calm herself before speaking. "You don't think I've done anythin'? You don't think my family has tried for generations to stop the creature? We've done *everythin'* we can. Why do you think this creature is only able to come out durin' the full moon?" I'm taken aback. I had assumed that its shapeshifting was voluntary, effected only by the moonlight. I had never thought to wonder if the shapeshifting was a way to prevent it from killing more people, but it all makes sense now.

"And you don't think Al has anything to do with this?" I ask.

"Al is harmless. He's been out there tryin' to keep kids safe from what lurks in that bayou. Tryin' to scare them away. But he can't be everywhere at once, and one day, I'm afraid, the beast may get him in its grip."

"So, then, how do we stop it? The monster?" I look at everyone at the table, but I'm only given blank stares.

A moment of silence passes before Mammy clears her throat and speaks up. "Cher, there is no way. Dark magic is too powerful. The curse will always find a way to endure."

I don't like this answer. I won't accept this answer, especially not when my friends' lives are in danger. When my life could be in danger. I don't care what Mammy says or anyone else. I will find a way to stop this monster and end the curse once and for all.

CHAPTER NINETEEN

"What do you know about curses?" I'm standing in front of Mr. C's desk after class. He looks shocked to see that I've stayed. My mind wasn't too focused on his lesson. All of the thoughts in my head are completely devoted to the Letiche and the curse. It's a wonder that I'm not failing all of my courses because of it.

I see Connor peek out behind the door from the hallway. He's stayed behind to eavesdrop on my conversation.

Connor has been indifferent to the investigation being back on. He still thinks it's a police matter, but he understands why Moira and I feel so strongly about helping Penelope and CeCe. He really didn't know how to react when I told him what Mammy had to say, but he seemed excited that Moira and I are friends again.

We haven't told the others, yet. Moira, Connor, and I still aren't on speaking terms with Valerie, Mabel, Greg, and Mark, but we do nod to each other from time to time when we see each other in the hallways or at lunch.

"Depends on the curse you're referring to." Mr. C takes his glasses off, gently setting them down. His eyes are a bright shade of green that aren't super noticeable when his glasses are on.

"The curse of the Letiche."

"Ah, so you've gotten to the part in your research with the curse?" He steeples his fingers and leans back in his chair.

"You've known there's a curse this whole time?" I slam my hands on the desk. Mr. C jolts in surprise, a tremor of shock making it all the way up to his eyebrows. Does every adult in Noir know about it? I reach up to stroke my pendant to keep me from another outburst, but then I remember that I left the necklace on my nightstand.

"Listen, Jensen, I know you've been through a lot, but I can't be giving you the answers for your essay. The point of this project is you doing the research yourself." Mr. C's face grows tight, the look of a parent scolding their child. "And the curse has been passed down through generations. Some Southern legend to keep kids in line. I'm sure everyone in Noir has heard of it at one point in their life. You probably have, too. You just..." Mr. C trails off, knowing he crossed a line.

"I just *forgot*. Is that what you were going to say?" My face feels flushed with heat, anger dripping from me in waves. Mr. C looks dumbfounded, like even he can't believe he let that slip.

"I'm so sorry—"

"Wait a second," I cut him off, my mind stuck on something he said. "I thought you just started working here. If you aren't from Noir, where did you hear about it?"

"I just moved to Noir, but it's a story all Southerners have heard. Plus, it's my job to know about legends and folktales. It's what I teach." He got me there. "Anyway, I have a meeting I have to get to. Keep up the good work. With more research, I'm sure you'll unlock other deep secrets of the South." Mr. C packs up his bag and darts out the door, sweeping right past Connor.

Connor steps through the door, an apologetic look on his face. I already know what he's going to say. He's going to want to apologize for what Mr. C said to me and I really don't want to hear it. "It's fine, Connor. I'm fine." I blow out a breath. Connor pulls me into a hug. It feels perfect being in his arms. "Thank you," I say, and it comes out in a small, breathy whisper.

Connor kisses the top of my head, a reminder of how much taller he is than me. "So, what are our next steps, detective?" He gives me a sly smile and that darn dimple makes an appearance.

There have been a lot of clues to process recently. I know

the Letiche is hunting in the bayou. I know that it's all because of some curse. I know that it walks around as a human, blending in with the rest of society. Unfortunately, my list of possible suspects is not much of a list. Al has been suspect number one for a while even though Mammy swears it can't be him. Now Mr. C is starting to look a little suspicious.

"We talk to Al."

ΔΔΔ

Finding Al is a lot different than finding any other person. After asking around, going door to door like evangelists, we learn that, yes, Al indeed owns a shack out here, but he rarely spends any time in it. He mostly hangs around outside in the woods and down by the bayou.

Connor and I walk aimlessly around the bayou, calling out every so often for Al.

"So, any sign of Penelope?" Connor breaks our silence. It's not that I don't want to talk to him, I've just been so focused on the task at hand: getting answers from Al.

"No, I haven't seen her. She might be too afraid to come around me."

"A ghost afraid of a human girl. Hm. That's a new one." Connor and I both start laughing. When he finally catches his breath he asks, "Penelope really doesn't know what did this to her? Or who? It'd really be helpful if she did."

I really do like Connor, but this question is getting exhausting. "Last we spoke, she had no idea who—or what—it was. She just knew she was attacked and that there is something out here killing people."

"If it is the Letiche, and the Letiche is a shapeshifting person, what are you going to do? Kill it?"

I hate the thought of killing anything, but I'll do what I have to do. "I'm going to stop it." I trip over a branch and stumble forward. Strong arms stop me from falling on my face. Strong arms that are forever etched in my memory.

I look to my left and see Connor standing there, fists up and ready to fight. Following the length of the arms wrapped around me, I look up and see the face of Al, his toothless grin greeting me.

I scramble out of his arms so fast and run behind Connor, trying to brush the grimy feel of him off me.

"Ya'll were callin' out fo' me. Ya act surprised I showed up." Al's Cajun accent is strong, making it hard to understand everything he's saying.

"People usually announce themselves first. They don't just pop up out of nowhere." Connor is still in his fighting stance, but I slowly move his fists down to his sides. We need to be on good terms with Al, no matter how bizarre he is, if we want to get answers. Connor relaxes a little, but he keeps me behind him. I'm not a helpless little girl, but I do appreciate how Connor wants to protect me.

Al leans against an old tree, crossing his dirt covered arms. His shirt is tattered and I can't tell if it's supposed to be grey or if it used to be white. The holes in his pants are all the way up to his thighs, incredibly thin to the point you can see his boxers underneath. My cheeks flush with embarrassment as I quickly avert my eyes from his lower half. It's not that you can see anything, but I don't want to be looking at an old, strange man's undergarments.

"So, whaddya want?" Al sticks his finger in his mouth, sucking the dirt out from under his nail.

I internally gag at the sight, but somehow manage to form words. "We're trying to stop the Letiche. We think it's the thing that's been killing all the kids, and we've heard you might know a thing or two about it."

Al spits out a wad of saliva that looks a little too much like tar. "And where ya hear that from?"

"Mam—I mean Geraldine James—er Lafayette. You went to school with her," I say.

"I know Geri. Goo' woman. Come on then." Al pushes off from the tree and stalks toward us. My heart hitches in my chest thinking that he's going to do something really bad to us. To my relief, he brushes by Connor and me, walking deeper into the woods and toward the bayou.

Down by the water is a tiny shack—house—with an outhouse right next to it. The yard, or what I assume is the yard, is covered in scrap metal and various wiring. The place resembles a junkyard more than it does a place to live. I glance around to see if there's a junkyard dog chained up somewhere waiting to bite at our heels.

"Watch where ya step. Got me some booby traps out here." Al swings his legs over a wire that's tied between two trees, and we copy his movements all the way to the front door. The crooked, wooden, front door looks like it's just leaned up against the frame. If a strong enough wind came through here, it'd probably blow the whole place down.

Al swings the door open and the smell that pours out of the house causes bile to build in my throat. Roadkill is the best way to describe the aroma. The scent of decay is so strong that I start to wonder if maybe it isn't the Letiche killing people after all. Maybe it is Al, and he's hiding the bodies somewhere underneath his shack. Maybe he's led Connor and I here because we're going to be his next victims.

Connor moves toward the threshold, and I grab his arm, halting his steps. Using my face, I try to convey to him that I don't think this is the best idea without having to say anything out loud for Al to hear. But Al catches sight of my worried expression and starts to laugh. "Ain't nothin' to worry 'bout, cher. No monsters up in here. Just me an' my critters." I look through the entrance into the main room of the house, the only room of the house, and I know what the smell is now. I also understand what he means by critters.

Al is heavily into taxidermy. There are dead animals hanging all over the place staring at us with lifeless eyes. A counter and sink rest against the wall to our left and both are covered in blood and guts, flies milling about the place looking for a good snack to land on. "Lemme open da window for ya. It's been so long since I've had guests. I get used to the smell, but I can see how it might be bothersome to you." Al politely opens the window in his tiny kitchen. The breeze rolls in, but it doesn't make the smell dissipate fast enough. I guess we'll just have to grin and bear it.

Al leads us to an old, yellow couch toward the back of the shack. The couch faces a wall that's covered in black and white photos, and various newspaper clippings. It's a little odd to have furniture facing a wall. I've only ever known furniture to face toward a television set. Al definitely has a different take on what he considers entertainment.

The couch is covered in dust and smells like it was left outside in the rain for a very long time, so long that the inside of the cushion is probably moldy.

"Would ya'll like a glass o' water?" Al takes a seat in a wooden chair across from us.

Thinking about what his glasses could potentially look like, I quickly, but politely, pass on the water and so does Connor. "Alrigh'. Suit yo'self. So, Geri pointed ya'll in my direction because ya think I know somethin' 'bout the Letiche?"

I lean forward on the couch, the smell starting to become overwhelming. "She said you moved out to the bayou because of it, and that you were trying to keep kids out."

Al points toward the wall with the photos and papers. I glance up and really focus on what's hanging there. All the photos and newspaper clippings are centered around the missing kids, but not just the ones missing from Noir, and not just kids missing from this year; it's decades of missing kids. One child every month dating back years ago. It's probably been going on even longer, there's just no newspaper reports on those kids.

Walking to the wall, I look at all their faces, wondering if one of them will reach out to me like CeCe did on the milk carton. None of them say anything or make any movements. They just stare back with their black and white faces and dead smiles. Headlines that talk about kidnappers, serial killers, and runaways grace the newspaper articles, all of which are lies.

"Ya know, people like Ted Bundy and Richard Ramirez have made it to where the cops don' think it can be anythin' else killin' these kids," Al says.

I look to Connor for some clarification. I have no idea who Ted Bundy or Richard Ramirez are. Connor clears his throat and says, "Serial killers." Ah. That makes sense.

"Then again, Satanic Panic got 'em all so worried that it could be the Devil takin' their babies." I've seen Satanic Panic plastered on the covers of magazines and newspapers my dad reads from time to time. Whatever it is, I know it's made my parents more involved in what Linda and I watch and read. It even had them concerned about us watching *Scooby Doo* for a period, but then my dad thought that was being too paranoid.

"So, you've seen the Letiche?" I ask.

"With my own two eyes. I chased it down once or twice, but it always disappears into the water."

"What does it look like?" I'm in complete awe that Al's actually seen the monster.

"Huge! Like a gator with the body of a giant, walkin' around on two legs or fo'. And its eyes blaze gold in the moonligh'." Just like the eyes Penelope saw.

Shivers make their way down my spine. As if alligators aren't scary enough, one with golden eyes and standing on two legs sounds awful.

Al walks to the couch, pushes Connor's legs aside, and leans down to fish something out from underneath it. He pulls a large hunting spear out, flipping it around in his hands, showing us how the tip of it gleams in the light. I exchange a look of concern with Connor. I'm feeling pretty uneasy about Al holding such a weapon, and, as nonchalantly as I can, I sit back down next to Connor. "This is wha' I plan to use on the sucker when I catch 'em."

"And you think that will—kill it?" Connor asks, his voice wavers.

Al shrugs his scrawny shoulders. "No, but it'll certainly slow it down."

"Do you know who the Letiche is? I mean its human form?" I ask. Connor folds his hands and props them under his chin, anticipating Al's answer. This whole thing will be so much easier if Al knows who the Letiche is. We may not even have to consider using his terrifying spear if we can track down the human.

My heart sinks, though, when Al shakes his head. "I scour tha' bayou all night long, until the wee hours of the mornin', but I ain't never seen no human walk up outta those waters."

Great. So, we're back to square one.

While Al has been able to give us some insight into what the monster looks like, I was really hoping he'd have caught who

AUDRAKATE GONZALEZ

it is.

My gaze travels back to the photos on the wall. "So, none of these people were ever found alive?"

Al has a somber look on his face. "No, cher. No bodies accounted for, either." It's so sad to think about all these families who will never have closure. CeCe's family will never get closure. Even if we're able to stop the Letiche, this isn't going to be a recovery mission. We'll never truly know where her final resting place is.

There's another picture on the wall that grabs my attention. It's so familiar that I instinctively reach for the pendant around my neck, even though I know it's not there. The photo is a sketch of my pendant. I reach up and trace the outline of it.

"Where did you find this picture?"

"I drew it myself. It's a sacred symbol tha's been used in my family for generations."

"Does your family have anything to do with the Letiche?" The Lafayette's were a part of banishing the Letiche to the darkness, maybe Al's family had some part in that as well.

"My pap from o'er a hundred years ago was in the tribe tha' cursed these parts. It's why I'm tryin' fix wha' they started. They never meant fo' it to get like this." Al points to me. "You recognize the symbol?"

"It—uh—it looks familiar to me. I might have seen it in a book before." I don't want Al to know I'm in possession of his family heirloom. He's already unpredictable. "What does the symbol mean?"

"The symbol was placed on a medallion made from the core of the earth tha' was cursed. The medallion was used as a conduit for the Letiche. It was the only power the tribe had o'er the monster. They not only used it as protection, but as a way to ensure the Letiche served its purpose."

Does this mean I can use my necklace to stop it? I absorb everything that Al has said and store it in my memory for later.

Connor gently tugs on my elbow. His eyes move to the open window, and I can see that the sun is starting to set. I'd like to get out of the bayou before it gets dark, and Connor clearly does, too. "Come on. Let's get out of here," Connor starts to lead me to the door.

"Ya'll be safe out there!"

As much as I was hoping an adult would be able to get involved in this situation, it looks like it's going to be up to me. And hopefully my friends will be by my side when I come face to face with the Letiche.

CHAPTER TWENTY

Parent-teacher conferences are by far the best thing to happen. Meetings between parents and teachers means a four-day weekend for all students, and the weather must have gotten the memo because the forecast reads sunshine all weekend.

To celebrate, I slept in this morning, not even bothering to wake before noon, watched some cartoons, and now I'm laying out on a beach towel in our front yard, sipping on a lemonade, rainbow one-piece on, and pencil and paper in hand. I've spent so much time figuring out how to stop the Letiche that I've completely neglected the essay I'm supposed to be writing about it.

Linda comes traipsing across the lawn, humming some ridiculous, annoying song that I'm sure she learned in school.

Something about Bumblebee Tuna and weird vowel sounds that follow. I wish I could rip my ears off. Maybe if I stick a for sale sign on her someone will come pick her up.

The sun is beaming down on me, and I can feel my skin starting to tingle. I should have put sunscreen on before I came out. After spending four years away from sunlight, my fair skin is no match for the rays. I'm sure I'll be the color of a tomato by the time I'm done, but I'm so focused on my essay that I can't be bothered by the sunburn that's creeping across my skin. Who knows, I might get lucky, and the burn will give me more freckles.

I've heard girls at school complain about their freckles, and I've seen how hard they try to cover them up with their mom's makeup, but I've never had a problem with my freckles. They give my face personality, and sometimes I wish they were a little bit darker.

"What are you doing, Jen?" Linda blocks the sun and takes all of its warmth with her.

I squint my eyes up at her, resisting the urge to instantly bite her head off. "I'm working on my homework so, if you could please quit distracting me, that would be marvelous." I feel my teeth clench together as soon as I close my mouth.

"That doesn't look like homework. That looks like something from *Scooby Doo*." Linda points to my *Shapeshifted* book, which is currently opened on a picture of the Letiche and some of the other shapeshifters. Since she's going to be so nosy, I may as well have fun with it.

"Actually, Linny," I use her nickname to make her feel at ease. She takes a seat next to me on my towel. "This is what's making all the kids disappear. It lives in the bayou and comes out to find the boys and girls who haven't been good, and it gobbles them up. On a full moon night, you can hear it roaming the streets, looking for the next bad child to snatch."

Linda's eyes are watery with fear, and just when I start to see the hairs raising on her arms, I add the final touch. "AH! Lin! The monster's right behind you!" I jump up from the towel, causing Linda to move just as fast. She whirls around toward the sidewalk in search of the monster. When she faces me, her eyes have released the water and tears are streaming down her cheeks.

Her face pinches, turning red with anger and embarrassment. "Oh, Jensen! You're mean, and ugly, and I *hate* you!" She pushes me back causing me to bump into my lemonade, spilling it all over my essay and the library book.

Well, as mad as I want to be, I deserved that. God must be getting a real good kick out of this one. Karma served.

I pick up the soaking book. Sweet, and sticky lemonade drips from its pages. "Linda, this wasn't my book! I borrowed it from the library."

"Well, you should have thought of that before you decided to be a jerk!" Linda sniffs.

"I didn't know you'd be such a chicken about it," I snap, shaking the excess lemonade from the book.

"I am not a chicken! I haven't been afraid of monsters in a long time. You just—you surprised me. That's all." Please. How many seven-year-olds do you know that aren't afraid of monsters? The answer is zero. All kids are afraid of monsters. And it just so happens that in Noir, they have every right to be afraid. But Linda doesn't need to know that the Letiche is real. If I told her, even if she'd believe me, it would only upset her.

"Whatever you say, Linda." I make a chicken sound, flapping my arms at my sides to emphasize that I know she's lying. I can practically see steam sprouting from Linda's ears as she marches back to the house.

Cleaning up my mess, I also head inside the house. I'm going to have to take the book back to the library and explain the whole thing to Donna. After my last visit to the library, I doubt that Donna likes me very much, and bringing in this ruined book will only solidify any opinions she may already have about me.

I change out of my swimsuit and throw on some of my more comfortable clothes. With the surprisingly nice weather, I decide on some baby blue, capris length leggings, and my oversized tie-dye t-shirt that I made a few months ago. There are swirling patterns on it of purples, pinks, and blues that I love.

I pull my necklace over my head, marveling at the symbol. I can't believe that this little necklace was used as protection. Then, I think about how I wasn't killed by the Letiche. As far as anyone knows, I've been the only survivor. Could it be because I was wearing this necklace?

I touch the scars on my head. I imagine sharp teeth grazing my skull, taking chunks along with them. Emotions swirl in my chest as I look in the mirror at the person I am while I think about what I could have been. I tuck the necklace safely in my shirt, and run my fingers through the hair I've mussed.

There's not really a whole lot I can do with my flaming, short hair. From being in the warm sun, my sweat has flattened any volume I had achieved earlier. It'll only get worse as the day goes on, no matter how much hairspray and teasing I do. Brushing it will have to suffice. I envy all the girls that have hair that stays full and voluminous amidst the Louisiana humidity.

Pulling out my blow dryer, I start to dry the book. I don't know how much good drying the book will do, but it can't make it any worse than it already is.

The pages have dried, but now they're discolored and wrinkly. Well, time to go get chewed out by Donna.

I place the book in my backpack, which barely fits because

of all the stuff that's still crammed in there, and walk to the library. It's not that far from my house, about a twenty-minute walk, but heat is making it feel like it's taking forever. It's the kind of heat that makes you feel sluggish, like you could curl up on the uneven sidewalk and take a nap, but I trudge on.

The library is busier than what I'm used to seeing. With the long weekend, I imagine many parents have sent their kids to the library while they're at work. Some of the kids I recognize from school, and it looks like they may be working on their assignments, using this long weekend as a way to catch up on all their work.

Donna is at the front desk, stamping books, glaring at all the students who have flooded her sacred library halls. She's probably used to the calm, quiet setting of the library. Today, it's a little rowdier than normal as friends meet up together to study, and Donna looks less than thrilled about this.

Walking up to the counter, I start rehearsing what I'm going to say to Donna in my head.

Hi there, I hope you're having a lovely day. My brat of a sister pushed me and I knocked lemonade onto this book that I borrowed. Please accept my sincerest apologies. Except, that doesn't sound sincere in my head, so I try the next one. *I am so sorry, but I accidentally spilled lemonade onto this book. I'll do anything to make it up to you. Just don't ban me from ever using the library again.*

Before I know it, I'm at the front desk having a stare down with Donna. I've been so busy trying to figure out what I'll say to her that I don't know how long I've been standing here like a zombie. I must look like a real creep.

"Can I help you?" Donna drawls in annoyance. Yeah, I'm for sure not her favorite customer.

With jittery hands, I place the ruined book on the counter. "I had a bit of an accident." I open the cover to show her the crinkled pages I tried to salvage. "The blow dryer saved it from falling apart, but I'm afraid the pages are permanently stained."

Donna puckers her lips, creating a loud smacking sound in the process. "We won't be able to put this back into circulation." Donna pivots toward the card catalogue behind her, and quickly shuffles her way through the stack. She takes out the card for *Shapeshifted* and slaps it on the counter in front of me. "That'll be twelve dollars," she says, her lips tight and voice flat. Well, there goes my monthly allowance.

I hand her the money, her face scrunching up when a few dollars' worth of change is dropped into her palm, but money is money and that's what I have. Donna stamps "Discarded" in big red letters across the title page. "It's yours now." She slides the book back to me and walks away, muttering under her breath something about irresponsible delinquents.

Making my way toward the exit, I spot Mr. C leaving out the same door in a hurry. Shouldn't he still be at the school? He must have finished his meetings early. Outside, the sun is starting to set. It must be a lot later than I originally thought.

I spot Mr. C jogging down the sidewalk, looking rather disheveled. I think about calling out to him but decide better of it. He clearly can't be bothered. I notice the way he brushes past the people walking in front of him, like they're slowing him down. I put my head down, trying not to draw attention to myself, and I follow him, wanting to know what the rush is.

The sun lowers more, painting pink and red streaks across the sky. Looking at the painted canvas is when I realize I can make out the appearance of the moon. It's going to be a full one tonight.

I peel my eyes away from above me to track Mr. C again. He's nowhere in sight. I do a three-sixty, but no sign of him anywhere. Darn it. Well, no use in staying out here any longer. It's getting dark, and with the full moon looming ahead, outside is the last place I want to be. Especially when I realize that I've followed Mr. C not too far away from the woods and the bayou beyond it.

The wind starts to blow, rustling the trees in front of me. Streetlamps flicker to life, their lights casting shadows in the fading daylight. There isn't a single person out here beside me, and I have a nervous feeling rest in the pit of my stomach. This is the perfect setting for the Letiche, and while I'm not exactly in its territory, I don't know how far it's willing to travel outside of the bayou for a late-night snack.

I need to get home.

A cold hand grasps my wrist from behind, sending an electric jolt through my body.

CeCe is standing behind me, her hair caked with mud, and dark red droplets stick to her face. Her eyes are rimmed with purple shadows, her skin as pale as snow. I see her mouth moving, like she's trying to say something, but her teeth just chatter together as though she's freezing cold. My heart lurches at the sight of her, images planting themselves in my brain as to what could have happened to her and where her body could currently be resting. From the look of her, I'd imagine she must be somewhere in the waters of the bayou.

Water bubbles up and out of her mouth, dribbling onto the ground in front of us. I take a step back so it doesn't splash on my shoes. "Your sister—" CeCe takes a deep breath, her lungs rattling, and tries again. "Your sister went into the bayou."

CHAPTER TWENTY-ONE

My eyes feel like they're going to pop right out of my head. There is no way that CeCe could mean that *my* sister went into the bayou. That can't be what I heard. She must be mistaken. Linda can barely tolerate being alone in her own room. She couldn't possibly be able to handle being in the bayou by herself. Especially when the sun is starting to fade into the horizon. It just doesn't make any sense.

I shake my head in denial to CeCe's claim. "You must have the wrong sister." I stroll past CeCe, heading toward town.

"Your sister's name is Linda. She has hair brighter than the sun and pulled up into a hot pink scrunchie. She has a flashlight in her hands, but I don't know how long the batteries are going to last." CeCe gives me a grave look, daring me to tell her she's wrong again.

"She wouldn't…" A loud gasp escapes me. I scared her with the story of the Letiche, and maybe I scared her just enough that she thought she had to prove something to me or simply prove something to herself. That she isn't afraid of the bayou or any monsters inside it. I'm the worst big sister in the world.

I move in the direction of the woods, the entrance of the bayou. CeCe, using her supernatural skills, appears in front of me, blocking me from entering. "What the heck, CeCe?"

"You can't go in there alone," CeCe warns.

"My sister is in there, so I most definitely *can* go in there alone." I maneuver around her, and then the weirdest thing that's ever happened to me happens; CeCe's ghost moves right through me. I don't see it happen, but I feel it. At first, I feel cold all over, like a bucket of ice has been dumped in my body. But then the coldness switches to a tingling that reminds me of when your foot falls asleep, except it's happening from my head to my toes. As CeCe passes through me to reach the other side, my breath is taken away with her, and I feel myself slowly crumple to the ground.

CeCe stands over me, water from her torn clothes dripping on me. "You can't go in there alone. The sky is clear. The moon will be full. It'll be hunting soon." CeCe looks all around as if the Letiche could be listening to us at this very moment. "You need to get the gang." She's referring to our group of friends. What she doesn't know is that the gang isn't much of a gang anymore.

"It's just me, Connor, and Moira now. The others don't want anything to do with us."

"They'll help you. I know they will." There's a reassurance in her eyes that gives me hope. "But you have to go now. The evil is ready to shift. I can feel it." CeCe quietly walks—er floats—to the bayou. "Penelope and I will watch your sister." She says that to make me feel better about leaving, but I'm not entirely sure how two ghosts are going to be able to protect my sister from an actual monster. But there's no time for me to sit here and think about that.

I push myself off the ground and head to the first place I can think of where I'll be able to easily gather my friends. Daley's Appliances.

△△△

Valerie is walking around the store, making sure things are in order for closing. Mabel is leaned over the counter flipping through a magazine, while Mark and Greg are plopped on top of washers waiting for Valerie to be done with work.

The bell dings as I burst through the door, announcing my arrival. I hear Valerie groan at the sound of the bell. "We're closing," she says, trying to sound polite, but I can hear the smoke of irritation creep through the cracks of her customer service voice.

"I need your help. And I need to use your phone."

They all look at me with shocked expressions on their faces. Mabel rushes over, spins me around, and starts to push me toward the door. "Nope. We're not dealing with you right now. You heard Valerie. The store is closing."

I swing my arms out to my sides, grabbing onto the doorframe, preventing Mabel from pushing me any further. "I need your help!" I shout, using all of my muscles against Mabel. She pushes harder. Dang, she's strong.

"You lost our help when you started acting like you were living in *The Twilight Zone*," Mabel grunts.

"I was telling you the *truth!*" I plant my feet harder, locking my knees as I feel Mabel press me into the handle of the door. She's lucky I need her help otherwise I'd be pulling her outside with me and onto the pavement.

"You're ridiculous!" Mabel seethes in my ear, and that's when I've had enough.

I thrust my elbow into her stomach, not enough to cause injury, but enough to catch her off guard and get her off my back. "My sister is out in that bayou, and if we don't go find her, she's going to end up just like CeCe and Penelope."

Mabel is breathing hard, but I notice her face soften when

she hears about my sister. The others are also giving me their full attention, Valerie standing with her hand over her mouth, and Greg and Mark slowly getting off the washers.

"Your—your sister is out there?" Tears well in Valerie's eyes.

I nod. "CeCe told me." My eyes flicker to Mabel, who looks like she wants to make a comment about CeCe talking to me, but she bites down on her lip instead. "Now, I need to use the phone, and I need you guys to put your feelings about me on the back burner because I need your help."

Valerie reaches over the counter, the phone in her hand, and I slowly take it from her. "Thank you," I say, already dialing Moira's number. Moira answers on the third ring.

"James's residence."

"Moira, I need you to get to Daley's Appliances as soon as possible."

"Jensen?"

"Yes. Look, Linda is in the bayou. CeCe told me. And it's a full moon!"

"Say no more. I'm on my way." The phone clicks. Valerie flips the sign on the door to "closed" and locks it. They gather around the front counter while I give them a breakdown of everything that they've missed out on.

"Wait, so Moira's grandma knows all about this too?" Mark

seems genuinely surprised to hear that a grown adult believes in something like the Letiche.

"And this thing could be anyone we know?" Mabel sounds concerned. A bang at the door causes us all to jump. Moira is standing outside frantically waving at us to let her in. Valerie runs to the door, unlocking, and letting Moira in.

"I called Connor before I left. He said he would meet us at the bayou." Moira grabs my arms. "Jensen, I'm really trying not to freak out, but I'm honestly freaking out." I don't have it in me to tell her that I'm freaking out too. Instead, I pull her into a hug because it's what I need.

"Flashlights are in my car. Let's go get Linda." Moira leads the way to her parked car. We pile in, Moira driving, and me in the passenger seat, the rest of the group crammed in the back. Moira's car is nowhere near big enough for all of us, but there's no time to worry about comfort. Moira jams the key in the ignition, and the engine roars to life. It isn't until Moira takes off down the street at alarming speeds that I wonder if she even has her driver's license.

"Moira, do you have—"

"Don't ask what you don't want to know." Meaning that Moira doesn't actually have a driver's license. Lovely. "Walk us through the plan, Jen." The plan? I haven't thought about a plan. I've only been thinking about finding my sister, getting her out of the bayou, and then giving her an earful on how she better never do something so stupid again. I haven't even thought about what we'll do if we happen to run into the Letiche. Now I feel sick. "Jensen, the plan?" Moira takes her eyes off the road, focusing on me. "Tell me you have a plan."

My brain shifts into overdrive. "Yeah—I—there's a plan." I unzip my backpack, pulling out frogging gear that I've never taken out. Two frog gigs and a net.

"You plan to go up against some alligator monster with a couple of frog gigs?" Greg sounds incredulous, and I don't blame him.

"No. We'll head to Al's shack first. He has a spear. Connor and I both saw it." That'll be the best protection we can get. "Once we get the spear, we go look for Linda. When we find her, we get the heck out of there." I turn in my seat, making sure to emphasize every word. "*No one* goes anywhere alone. We don't split up. Understood?" I get a nod from each of them, and then I turn back to the windshield as Moira pulls into the entrance of the woods.

CHAPTER TWENTY-TWO

Moira shifts the car into park, right next to Connor's Pinto. I scramble out of the car to get to Connor, but he's not outside. I shine my flashlight over the car. His front seat is empty. At first glance, the window seems to be rolled down, but then I notice the shards of glass littering the ground next to the car. On the driver's side door there's long, deep gashes across the metal. There's a dark puddle next to the glass. I avert my gaze from it, trying not to think what that dark puddle is or what it could mean.

I march back to Moira's car like a woman on a mission. "We have to move now." My voice is firm even though I'm shaking all over.

"What's wrong?" Valerie's voice is raised and laced with fear.

"Where's Connor?" Moira asks.

I'm moving through the woods with everyone else trying to keep up behind me. The beam of my flashlight is sporadically moving in every direction. I can't help but feel like the Letiche is going to jump out from the darkness at any moment. "Connor is missing. His car—" I gulp loudly. "His car was attacked." Someone behind me sucks in air, like they're trying to conceal their crying. I bet it's Valerie. She's just as emotional as CeCe was.

The bayou is always creepy. There's nothing that could make it not creepy. But tonight, knowing that it's a full moon, knowing what is out here with us, makes it the scariest place on earth.

The breeze blows through the trees, sounding like the soft whisper of lost souls. I can almost hear them begging us to leave before it's too late. Frogs croak in the distance, agreeing with the wind. The moonlight peaks through the trees occasionally, bathing parts of the woods in an indigo hue. It only makes the shadows stand out more. Human shaped silhouettes sneaking behind the trees, hiding when our flashlights pass by. Maybe it's my imagination, or maybe it's more innocent ghosts who were killed by the Letiche.

Al's shack is looming in the distant. We all run over and duck behind a group of nearby barrels, which is either part of his garbage pile or simply his yard aesthetic. From the window we can see that there are no lights on, not that I think Al has electricity anyway. With the full moon tonight, I don't have any worries that Al will be inside. He's probably running around the bayou looking for the Letiche. My fingers are crossed that he's left the spear behind.

"I'll go in. You guys wait here." I stealthily move away from the barrels, but Mabel grabs my arm before I can get too far.

"Shouldn't we all go together?" she asks. I know I originally said we shouldn't split up and no one goes anywhere alone, but this is different. Al has a bunch of booby traps all over his yard, and I'm the only one who has seen them. It'll be a lot easier for me to navigate his maze on my own without having to worry about the others.

"I won't be long."

"What if his door is locked?" Greg is serious, and we all do a double take from the dilapidated shack to Greg. He throws his hands up in defense. "Okay, okay. He probably doesn't lock his door." With my friends semi-reassured, I make my way toward Al's shack.

I keep my flashlight close to the ground paying careful attention to all the traps. Unfortunately, I miss the fishing wire that blends in with the rest of the ground. My shin hits it with just the right amount of pressure, pulling a net of cans to the ground and creating a raucous sound. Ducking into a ball, I cover my ears and wait for the noise to pass, praying to God that the sound was contained to this small bubble and didn't spread throughout the rest of the bayou.

A quick glance toward my friends tells me that the sound most definitely travelled. Their faces all display varying looks of horror. Well, if I wasn't in a hurry before, I am now.

Zooming through the rest of the tall grass and booby traps, I stretch my legs out and make a long leap toward the top of stairs. My tennis shoes slip a little when they connect with the step, but I swiftly catch myself, grasping the banister with my outstretched hand just in time.

The door of the shack swings open with a gentle shove. I knew Al wouldn't lock his door. It's pitch-black inside. Even darker than the woods. The floorboards creak under my feet as I make my way through the inky black room. My flashlight illuminates the couch, and something shiny reflects at me from underneath. Hallelujah. The spear!

As if I'm a baseball player sliding into home, scoring that last point and winning the game, I dive across Al's floor to take my prize. And from the stab of pain I get in my stomach; I realize that sliding on these old wooden floors is not my brightest moment. I'm not looking forward to having to pull these splinters out later. Then again, if the Letiche crosses my path these splinters will be no big deal.

I drag the spear out from its hiding place, reveling in the feel of it in my hands. I've never felt more powerful. I'm a warrior ready to go into battle. A warrior that's ready to fight anything away from my sister. Hopefully Al won't be too mad at me for borrowing the spear. Fingers crossed that nothing happens to the spear and I can return it to its home before Al even knows that it's gone.

Bolting out the door, I'm reminded of all the times I've heard my mom yelling at Linda not to run with sharp objects. One time, not too long after I came home from the hospital, Linda was running with a pair of scissors. She tripped and fell, clipping her ear in the process. It bled a lot, but nothing was damaged to the point of needing a trip to the emergency room.

It didn't matter, though. My mom still freaked out, screaming at the sight of Linda's blood on the carpet. I could just imagine how much she would freak out now as I run across Al's yard with a giant spear in my hands.

Mark's eyes go wide at the sight of the spear, and he lets out a low whistle. "Al wasn't messin' around!"

A blood curdling scream ricochets across the bayou. It's the sound of pure terror and coming from a little voice I know well. Linda. She may be small, but she sure does have a set of pipes on her.

The six of us take off toward the source of the sound,

but with all the other noises of the bayou, and the darkness shrouding in, it's too hard to identify where Linda could be.

"Linda!' I scream at the top of my lungs, running blindly. I hear Moira shout Linda's name from somewhere behind me, and then the rest of the group joins in. "Linda!" I can taste blood in my mouth.

Penelope's ghostly figure stops me in my tracks. She looks like she's about to cry, her lips quivering. "Jen, it found her!"

CHAPTER TWENTY-THREE

"Where is she?!" I scream at Penelope. Moira runs into my back while everyone else stands next to her, none of them able to see Penelope.

A roar echoes around us, deep, inhuman, and guttural. A sound that would make any grown man run in the opposite direction. My hand shoots up to my scars, and Penelope's own hand moves to the wounds on her head. A tingling sensation laces itself across my skull. My friends crowd around me, clearly all shaken by what's going on.

We all jump at the sound of a car horn.

"She's by the cars!" I run right through Penelope as she starts to fade away.

The last time I remember being scared was when I woke up in a hospital room all by myself. I didn't know who I was. I didn't know where I was. It was the feeling of being utterly alone in the world and completely forgotten. But even the fear that jolted through me the day I woke up is nothing compared to the fear I feel coursing through my veins right now. Adrenaline is the only thing keeping me from passing out at this point. Adrenaline and worry that if I pass out now, if I chicken out now, something terrible is going to happen to my sister. I grip the spear tighter, preparing myself for whatever lies ahead.

Moira's car comes into view, and the blaring horn gets louder. I run up to the driver's door, relief in my chest at the sight of Linda in the front seat, wailing on the horn. Tears are raining down her cheeks, her hot breath fogging the windows. She doesn't let off the horn, and it isn't until I knock on the glass that she even notices I'm there.

Linda screams again, thinking I must be the monster that's been chasing her. She bawls at the sight of me. Her big sister coming to the rescue.

"Linny, I need you to open the door for me, okay?" She locked it to protect herself, and Moira is still fumbling around trying to dig the keys out of her pocket.

Linda sucks in her lip. "You have to hurry, Jenny. It's still out there!" Linda's shaky hands reach for the lock, but movement from the shadows makes her freeze. In fact, we all turn into statues, our muscles tensing. I bring the spear up, leveling it with my eyes, poised like a gladiator.

It's the first time all night that the bayou becomes deathly silent. It's as if every living creature has fled to safety, and we're the only ones stupid enough to stay behind.

A deep rumble comes, making my legs shake, and out of the darkness two glowing circles appear.

Eyes.

The eyes of the Letiche.

"Uh, Jensen, let's get in the car please," Valerie's voice is soft and frightened. Moira, finally getting her fingers to work properly, manages to get the keys from her pocket, but she drops them in the dirt, causing Mark and Greg to dive in search of them. I don't take my gaze away from the glowing eyes floating in the gloom.

Mark finds the keys, but it's too late. The monster jumps out of the shade and lands right in front of us—all seven feet of it. A mixture of dark green scales and brown matted fur covers its body. The legend was not wrong; this is a monster born of the devil and raised by gators.

The face of the creature resembles an alligator, but only from the nose up. I can see how easy it would be for it to blend in with other gators in the water. Its jaw is angular, much like that of a human, but its teeth are all gator, sharp and dangerous. Its tail swings out from behind it, adding at least another four feet to its body. Claws jut out from its webbed feet, gleaming in the light of the moon, ready to swipe. It stands in front of us on two legs, but then slowly crouches down to all fours, in a position to attack.

I mimic the stance, crouching down, and hold the spear out to keep distance between us. Moira takes the keys from Mark, and she runs to the other side of the car with Valerie and Mabel following close behind. Greg and Mark join my battle stance, flanking me on either side, both holding a frogging gig as a weapon. I doubt it will do much damage to something as monstrous as the Letiche, but at least it's something.

The passenger door opens and I hear Linda's protests at the door no longer being locked. The girls pile in the car with Linda, calming her shouts, and Mabel shuts and locks the door behind her. All of them stare at us from the foggy windows.

"Get out of here!" I silently mouth to Moira, who is now sitting in the driver's seat. She nods in my direction and jams the key into the ignition. At the sound of the car turning over, the Letiche roars, sending saliva flying in every direction. With a great burst of speed, the monster charges toward us. I scamper backward, my back now pressing against Moira's car. Mark and Greg are much braver than I am. They charge forward, heading straight for the Letiche.

Mark makes a move to jump onto the beast, but it catches sight of him before Mark's feet barely lift the ground. My breath catches in my chest as I watch the Letiche whip its body around, sending its tail straight toward Mark. I want to shout, but I can feel the noise sticking in my throat. It wouldn't matter even if I did shout. There was no warning I could give Mark because it would be too late.

The monster's tail connects with the center of Mark's body.

I feel as though I'm watching everything happen in slow motion. Like in one of those action films my dad always enjoys watching. The fight scenes happen slowly so that the audience can take in every move. I feel as if I could be watching one of those movies now, and not seeing my friends get hurt. Then Mark's body flies through the air from the impact. His back connecting with the car, making a sickening *crunch*, and he slides to the ground, completely limp.

Horrified screams come from inside the car. The girls all call out to Mark, but he is silent. I feel like I should be screaming too. Afterall, Mark's limp body is slouched over right next to me, but I don't do anything other than stare at him and then back to the Letiche.

The beast stalks Greg but, after seeing what happened to Mark, Greg has enough sense to not charge after it. It looks like a game of cat and mouse. Greg moves from one side to the other, and the Letiche copies his movements.

With the Letiche now distracted by Greg, Moira tries again to start the car. It turns over a couple of times, but the car never sputters to life. It's possible that someone, or something, tampered with the car while we were at Al's shack.

Moira is banging on the steering wheel, curses spewing from her lips about the car and her bad luck.

I watch as Greg gets close enough to jab the frog gig at The Letiche. He misses, and the Letiche bats him away with his giant webbed foot. I hear the smack of the foot against Greg's chest, and I see Greg roll off into the underbrush.

With those two taken care of, there's only one more threat left to the Letiche.

Me.

CHAPTER TWENTY-FOUR

Yellow, glowing eyes flick from me to the spear in my hand, trying to gauge how best to take me down. I've got news for this monster; I won't be taken down easily. There's too much at stake for me. Not just my life, but the lives of my friends, my sister, and not to mention avenging Penelope, CeCe, and all the other kids the Letiche has taken away too soon.

I take the spear and stab the air by the Letiche, just barely missing its scaly side. In a fury, the Letiche lunges toward me snapping its jaws at my legs. The sound of its jaw slamming shut, its teeth gnashing together, and my leg thankfully just out of reach, is enough to send me scrambling toward the car.

I pull myself onto the hood, and make my way to the roof. Even when I get to the roof I won't have any height advantage, but I'll at least be eye to eye with the monster. Muffled shouts from the car tickle my ears. At first, I think they're all cheering for me. It isn't until I really focus on their shouts that I realize what they're saying.

"Behind you!!"

I turn my head just in time to see sharp claws swinging in my direction. There's not enough time for me to dodge them, so I turn my back to them instead. The claws drag down my back, shredding my shirt and taking skin along with it. I scream in pain as hot liquid oozes from the marks left behind on my body. It hurts so bad, but I know I've survived worse. The scars on my head tingle in response to that thought. The Letiche thought it had me before, and probably thinks it has me now, but I am a force to be reckoned with.

I suck up the blaring pain in my back and use it as fuel for my adrenaline instead, and I shift to face the Letiche. I grit my teeth together, feeling one tooth chip in the process. If—no, *when* —I survive this, I'll be making a trip to my dad's office.

A battle cry rips from my throat. I jump from the roof of the car, the spear positioned above me ready to penetrate my enemy. The Letiche goes from four legs to two and catches me midair. It smells awful up close. It reeks of dead, rotting fish roasting in humid, summer heat.

In the close proximity, it's hard to maneuver the long

spear, but that doesn't stay a problem for long. The Letiche moves its face closer. I hold the spear out to the side between us, preventing the Letiche from chomping down on my head. It gets a mouthful of spear instead, snapping the spear in half. Before the side with the sharp point can drop to the ground, I catch it, flip it over, and stab the Letiche right in its yellow eye.

The beast howls in pain and drops me to the ground. The air whooshes out of my lungs as I land. Dirt floats up all around me causing me to choke when I try to breathe again. From the impact, my eyes are all hazy, but I'm able to make out the shape of the Letiche retreating to the dark woods.

The car door opens and Mabel, Valerie, and Moira split up to check on the condition of the guys. Tiny arms wrap around my side. I wince as the little arms squeeze. With all the adrenaline leaving my body, my aches hit me with full force. Linda looks up at me, tear stains streaking her cheeks.

"Jenny, I'm so, so sorry. I just wanted to be brave. I wanted to show you I wasn't afraid of anything. It wasn't bad at first, but then it got darker, and I saw an alligator in the water, but then it came out of the water, and it wasn't an alligator at all!" Linda talks so fast that I can barely make out her words.

"Shh," I coo. "It's not your fault. I should have never told you that story in the first place. I'm the one who should be saying sorry." Linda curls up into my lap. She seems so small and frail, and even though I'm sore all over, I don't move her. If only my parents could be here to see this.

There's some rustling from the trees where the Letiche made its exit. Linda whimpers. I use all my remaining strength to pull myself up and shield Linda behind me. Linda hands me a frog gig she finds on the ground. I watch Mabel silently place Mark in the car. He must be okay, but he's definitely going to need to get to a hospital soon.

From the woods, the shadow of a man comes into view. Mr. C is unsteady on his feet as he makes his way closer to us. His clothing is tattered and torn. Blood is dripping down from a wound on his head, right above his eyebrow. I push Linda up against the car and brandish the frog gig in front of me.

"Don't come any closer!" I yell at Mr. C. It all seems too suspicious that Mr. C would arrive all beat up right after I kicked the Letiche's butt. I don't know who the Letiche is when it's in human form. I can't trust Mr. C coming anywhere near us.

"Jensen, please, it's just me. You know me. Mr. C." He sounds pathetic. "Put down the weapon, please. I was attacked by the creature. I need help." He looks from me and Linda to Mabel and Mark. "I can see you need help, too. Let's go get help together." He takes another step closer to us.

There's some movement to my left. I shift my gaze in that direction, but not enough to completely lose sight of Mr. C. Moira and Valerie come out of the woods holding Greg up between them. He's pretty beat up. Gashes and bruises are on his face and arms. His eye looks like it may be swollen, but at least he's alive. I breathe a sigh of relief at that.

Mr. C takes a step in their direction.

I wave the gig around, getting his attention again. "I said *don't come any closer!*" My voice is rich with vehemence, but I can feel tears pricking my eyes. This night has already been a lot to take, but the thought of having to fight my teacher off is putting me over the edge.

"Jensen, please." There's a softness in his voice that makes me want to silence the alarm bells ringing in my head. The sound is soothing like a lullaby, reassuring like a friend, and all together trustworthy.

Which is exactly why I can't trust it at all. I grip the frog gig tighter, causing my knuckles to blanche, and I narrow my eyes. "If you take one more step, I will—" I don't get to finish my warning as the Letiche tears out of the dark heading straight toward Mr. C.

CHAPTER TWENTY-FIVE

Mr. C screams in pain as the Letiche clamps its jaws down on his arm and thrashes him around like a rag doll. The scene is horrific as blood spurts from Mr. C and rains down all around us. I must be in some state of shock, though, because the sight of the blood isn't making me queasy. Linda gasps behind me. I forgot she's witnessing the same horror that I am, and while there's a lot about this night she'll never forget, this isn't something I want scarring her for life.

"Linny." Her big eyes meet mine. "I need you to turn around and close your eyes. Whatever you hear, don't open them." She obediently shuts her eyes and turns around, holding her hands over her ears for extra measure. Good girl.

When I spin back around, the Letiche is gone. Mr. C is on the ground. I don't know if he's alive or...dead. I can't just leave him there. I have to check.

I move toward him, checking my surroundings as I go. Mr. C is on his side. His marred arm is limp over his stomach. The skin of his arm is just ragged strips. Chunks of flesh are strewn on the ground around him. I think I see jagged white poking through the gaping muscle of his arm.

Bone.

I swallow the bile that's inching its way up my throat. It leaves an acrid aftertaste in the back of my mouth. Avoiding the ruined arm, I slowly turn Mr. C's body over. He groans, and his eyelids flutter but don't open. It's enough confirmation for me that he's alive, but not conscious.

Moira leaves Valerie and Greg and kneels next to me.

"Is he going to be okay?" Clearly, he's not in good shape at all and, like Mark and Greg, he needs medical attention as soon as possible, but Moira is too scared to answer that question herself. She needs my reassurance.

"He's going to be fine." I really don't know, but I tell the lie anyway. "We just need to get him out of here quickly, and carefully." Moira and I slip our arms underneath Mr. C's body to lift him. We're going to have to get him into the car so we can get him out of here. Then Moira drops him and scrabbles back.

I'm about to yell at her, but then I see a tear trickle down her cheek, and her lips quiver. She lifts a finger, pointing behind me, and my face goes slack realizing what she could possibly be pointing at.

The Letiche is crouched right next to Linda, saliva dripping from its mouth. She's still facing the car, eyes squeezed shut and hands over her ears. She has no idea about the monster that's by her side.

I gently roll Mr. C back onto his side and take my frog gig. I don't know how this is going to end. This isn't some episode of *Scooby Doo* where I have an elaborate trap that ensnares the villain. *Where's Fred when you need him?* This won't end by me simply unmasking the monster. The only thing I can be sure of is that whatever happens, it's not going to involve my little sister getting hurt. Not if I can do anything about it.

As stealthy as a predator, I jump onto the Letiche's back. The beast lurches, taking me on the ride of a lifetime. I hang on with all the strength I have left in my body, which isn't much, but it's enough to keep me from flying off its back. Linda, sensing the commotion going on, opens her eyes and whips her head around.

"Linda!" I scream, gripping the oily fur of the Letiche tighter. "Run!" Linda's legs must be too scared and weak because she shakes her head and crawls under the car instead. Well, at least she's not out in the open.

The Letiche's arms reach behind to try and claw me off,

but thankfully its arms aren't long enough to get a good swipe. Taking the gig, I stab the Letiche's back, but the gig can't break through the armor like scales. This is just fan-freaking-tastic. I make a move to stab the monster in the eye again, but the Letiche knows this move since that's where I attacked the first time. We spin, and the next thing I know my body is being slammed up against Moira's car. The car shifts backwards from the force, exposing Linda's hiding spot, and sending Mabel into a fit of screams.

The clash of my body against the car causes something within me to crack. White hot pain laces its way up my body. I lose my grip on the beast and fall to the ground, the frog gig rolling away from me. The Letiche looms over me, a triumphant gleam in its eyes. A low growl escapes its throat as it moves its body directly over mine, coming face to face.

I turn my head away from it, not wanting to face my death. Penelope and CeCe come into view, and I wonder if there will be someone else out there that will be able to see and hear me once I die.

Penelope smiles. "Not today, Jensen." What? What could she mean? Of course it's today. The Letiche is literally standing over me ready to devour. I can feel its hot breath on my face. I look up into the eyes of the monster. It takes its long, slimy tongue and traces my skin. I shut my eyes to the feeling, and I open them again to see the reason why today will not be the day.

A familiar shape is scarred onto the chest of the Letiche. An archaic sun; a circle with beams fanning out in every direction. I survived this monster once before, the scars on my head are proof of that. It's always been a wonder as to how I was able to survive. What stopped the creature that attacked me from finishing the job? But now I have my answer.

As the beast's face inches closer, I rip the pendant from around my neck and slam it against the scar on the Letiche. With a guttural roar, the Letiche staggers away from me. Light protrudes from its body, ricocheting throughout the air, brightening the bayou. Birds scatter from the trees, and other animals scamper across the ground as the bright light stirs them.

The blazing light fades. A body lies on the ground, one that I recognize, and I feel my heart split right down the middle.

Where the Letiche once stood is now where Connor lies. I run over to him, choking on a sob. I hate the monster for what it has done, but it has never once crossed my mind that the monster could be someone I truly care about.

"You stopped the curse." Connor gives a hoarse laugh, and then sputters. Black ooze leaks from his lips.

I can't do anything other than cry.

"Don't shed tears for a monster. I would have killed you.

I would have killed all of you." His head rolls back, and Connor doesn't speak again. His eyes are vacant. The spot where the scar once was is completely charred, like the pendant burned right through his skin. I reach out to touch him, to see if there is any life left, but his body starts to shrivel, turning to dust before my eyes.

A child born of the devil.

The floodgates open as tears fall from my eyes uncontrollably. They're a mixture of relief and sadness. Relief that this night is finally over, that the curse is broken, and we'll never have to deal with the Letiche again. Sadness for who—what—Connor turned out to be.

"They're through here!" I hear someone yell. Al comes through the woods leading a team of police officers and paramedics. My body sags at the sight of the paramedics rushing to help my friends. A few of the officers radio in on their walkies. Before I know it ambulances and police cruisers are pulling in. They load Mr. C, Mark, and Greg up onto gurneys.

One of them rushes over to me and asks me a bunch of questions. Everything is pretty hazy, though, and I know the paramedic realizes I'm not okay when I don't answer any of the questions coherently. I'm loaded up onto a gurney, strapped in, and hoisted into the back of an ambulance. The sterile smell burns my nose, and I can feel my heart accelerate as I think about the last time I woke up in a hospital.

I frantically pull at the straps, trying to undo all the little buckles across my stomach. My ribs are screaming at me to stop. I think a couple of them may be broken. But I have to get out of this ambulance.

"Miss, it's all going to be okay." A paramedic gently removes my hands from the straps, but I swat her away.

"No, I—I can't go to the hospital," my voice cracks.

A small hand takes my own, and I see a smile break through the dirty face of Linda. "It's okay, Jenny. I'll be with you the whole time." And then, knowing Linda will make sure I wake up, I let the blackness sweep over me as I pass out.

CHAPTER TWENTY-SIX

In the coming weeks, I heal up rather nicely. My ribs still have a few more weeks of healing to go. In my fight with the Letiche—er Connor—I broke three ribs. The doctor said six to eight weeks and I would be back to normal. I only had to spend two days in the hospital, and true to her word, Linda stayed the entire time. She refused to go home with my parents, begging them to let her spend the night with me instead.

Linda is okay. She's more emotionally damaged than physically. But through this horrible experience, we've grown closer, so we will get through it together.

Mark and Greg are both going to be okay. Mark sustained some pretty bad injuries, and it will be a few more weeks before he sees the outside of the hospital room. Greg, like me, suffered a few scrapes, bruises, and a couple broken ribs. He's already relaxing at home, working on healing.

Mr. C is the one who got the worst of the Letiche's rage. The doctors weren't even sure he would make it at first. He had lost a lot of blood, and he'd gone into a deep state of shock. He's pulled through, but it'll be a while before he's able to resume his teaching position. In fact, there's rumors that he won't be back for the rest of the year. That's why Moira and I are visiting him in the hospital today.

I didn't get the chance to apologize to him. A big part of me feels like it's my fault he got attacked in the first place. If I had just believed him, maybe we could have avoided the rest of the events of that night. Then again, that would mean Connor would still be prowling around the bayou as a monster in the full moon. There's a con to every pro.

There are also other reasons for my visit to the hospital today. The main reason being to find out exactly why Mr. C was in the bayou that night in the first place.

Mr. C is laid up in his bed, wires attached to him, arm in a cast, channel surfing. He stops on an alligator documentary, staring at the images for a few moments before he shuts it off entirely. He catches sight of Moira and I in the doorway, balloons and a card signed by students in our hands. He smiles. "Hi girls. Come on in."

We do as he says and take seats in the only two chairs in

the room. Moira sets the card and balloons down on a table next to his bed before taking her seat.

"What brings you two here?" Mr. C asks.

"Well, actually, I wanted to start by apologizing. If I would have just listened to you, I could have probably saved us all a lot of trouble."

Mr. C shakes his head. "No need to apologize, Jensen." Silence follows. I feel grateful that he doesn't blame me, and I need a moment to just take it in.

Moira clears her throat. "Sir, we also wanted to ask what you were doing out there in the bayou that night."

Mr. C sits up a little straighter, wincing at the movement. "I guess it's time I'm honest with you kids, especially considering I won't be back in school this year. As a cryptid enthusiast, I came to Noir looking for something more than just a teaching job. I came here for the Letiche."

"But the Letiche was just a myth. I mean, at least at first. What made you think it was really here?" I ask.

"The cryptid community is small, but we all still talk and swap information from time to time. There had been plenty of sightings of the Letiche throughout Louisiana, but up until recently the sightings were sporadic. Then, within the last four years, we noticed a connection between all the missing kids and the Letiche. Noir was the epicenter. So, I got myself a job at the high school, and spent my free time hoping to capture a glimpse of the Letiche. Al was helping search that night, giving me a rundown on the bayou. I was attacked by the Letiche when I was with Al. He took off to get help for me. When I came to, I heard you kids screaming." Mr. C looks at his wrapped-up arm. "I guess I got a little more than I bargained for."

"So, are you going to tell your cryptid friends about this?" I'm not entirely sure how well that will work out for us and the story we spun with the police. As far as the police know, Connor was killed by a gator, and that gator attacked the rest of us as well. The police are hunting the supposed gator still. A team of them head out on a boat every day just scanning the bayou waters for this giant alligator we told them about. It won't look too good if a group of cryptid enthusiasts start poking around.

To my relief, Mr. C shakes his head. "No, I think that information is best kept to ourselves." Mr. C takes a deep breath. "So, Connor's family? How are they taking all of this?"

Moira looks at me to make sure I'm okay. I nod to her, signaling that she can take over this part of the story. It's still hard for me to talk about Connor.

"His family...they don't exist. Police checked and turned up nothing. Connor's home address? Fake."

"But—but that can't be true. I met his dad at the parent teacher conference." We all share a wide-eyed glance. The police said there was no trace of a family, but what Mr. C is saying does make sense. Moira said when Connor showed up it was four years ago, when he would have been in the eighth grade. There's no way he would have been able to sign himself up for classes without a parent around. Hopefully this is something the police are able to figure out. I've done enough investigating to last me a lifetime.

"I'm sure it's just a mistake on their part. They'll find his family soon enough." Mr. C sounds so positive, but I don't feel so sure.

At this point in the conversation, Mr. C's nurse steps in and informs us that he needs to get some rest. We wish him well and head home.

Moira got her driver's license after everything that night. Thank goodness, too. Her driving is much improved, and now I don't feel like I'm putting my life on the line every time I get in the car with her.

"So, what do you think about all that stuff Mr. C said about Connor's family?" Moira must be really bothered by what he said because she usually doesn't talk about Connor in front of me.

"I'm not sure what to think. Obviously, Connor's whole entire life was a lie, and he used that lie to get close to all of us."

"Do you think he knew he was the Letiche the whole time?" Moira asks.

"I think some part of him knew, and probably cared, but I think the evil side of him was stronger and prevented him from telling anyone who he truly was. You heard him. He would have killed all of us." That stops the conversation, and the trip to my house continues in silence.

Linda greets me at the front door with a big smile on her face. "You're never going to guess what I helped mom make!" The aroma of the house is delightful. I can tell they've been in the kitchen making some confectionery goodness.

"What's that, Linny?" I ask. Linda takes my hand and drags me to the kitchen. The kitchen is a mess of pots, pans, spoons, and batter. Resting on the stove is a platter piled high with the most amazing sight I've seen in weeks.

"Blueberry muffins! All for you!" Linda's body wiggles with excitement. I pick a muffin from the top and take a big bite out of it. It tastes better than ever.

EPILOGUE

Summer has set in, and the Louisiana heat is relentless even at night. Mark was finally given the okay by his parents and doctor to get out of the house. As a way to celebrate Mark's new freedom, my group of friends have decided to go to the roller rink.

The indoor rink smells like sweaty feet, pizza, and cigarettes. A lovely combination. The music is pounding through the multicolored, carpeted floor outside of the rink. It's dark, the only light coming from that of strobe lights, and glow sticks that various skaters wear on their bodies. Laughter mixes with the music, and it's the sound of everyone having a great time.

My friends and I skate until are legs are so sore, our feet are numb, and bruises coat our knees and butts from the amount of times we've fallen on the wooden rink. It isn't until a Phil Collins song begins to play, causing a happy memory of Connor to dance in our minds, that we put up our skates and head out the door. It's midnight, and the full moon is high in the crystal-clear sky. The humidity of the night makes my clothes stick to my already sweaty body.

"Hey, what do you guys say we go to the bayou? You know, for old time's sake?" Mark asks. I want to immediately shut down that suggestion, but tonight we're celebrating Mark, and if that's what Mark wants to do, then that's what we're doing.

We walk in silence to the bayou. No goofing off. No lighthearted conversation. Just crickets. I imagine we're all thinking about the same thing; the last time we were in the bayou on a full moon night.

The bayou looks the same, minus the terrifying monster. We're the only things in the bayou that have changed. Moira and I are best friends. We do everything together. Nails, shopping, hair salon, even taking Linda with us when we can.

Mabel and Mark are *finally* together. We all knew it would happen eventually, but Mabel was defiant at first. It wasn't until Mark's run in with the Letiche that Mabel realized how much she cares about him.

Greg quit football which was a huge surprise to everyone. We all thought he loved it, that he dreamed of being an NFL football star one day. Turns out that's not true. Greg wants to be a surgeon of all things. Even his family was surprised when he quit. But we can all see how much happier Greg is now that he doesn't have to worry about sports.

Valerie started teaching self-defense classes at the school. She's there twice a week, leading girls our age on defense moves and mechanisms to keep them safe. She often wonders, had CeCe known self-defense, if it would have helped save her at all.

I haven't seen my ghost friends since that night. My scars haven't tingled at all again, either. It's my sign that they've truly moved on. Destroying the Letiche set their souls free. I'd be lying if I said I didn't miss them, but I also know they weren't going to be able to stick around forever. It wouldn't have been fair to them.

Mark picks up a stone, chucking it into the inky waters. "For all of our friends who can't be here today," he solemnly says. We all follow suit, all taking turns chucking stones into the water and commemorating our friends.

The underbrush behind us rustles, and we all jump. We turn, staring at the dark bushes. Out walks an alligator. It slowly makes its way toward the water. As a group we step back, making sure we're out of its way. My parents always say if you don't mess with them, they won't mess with you.

"Let's get out of here," Mabel suggests. My friends make

their way up the small incline to Moira's car.

I follow them, carefully passing the alligator with plenty of distance between us. As it moves on by, it slightly turns its head to give me a sideways glance. In the pale moonlight, I see the yellow eye of the gator wink at me, and then it moves into the water. A chill inches its way through my body, and my feet cannot get me to the car fast enough.

THE LEGEND OF THE LETICHE

When I decided to have the second book of the *This is Noir* series take place in Louisiana, I knew it had to have the perfect monster. I did a lot of research on cryptid legends in Louisiana. Most of the stories were about the Honey Island Swamp Monster, Rougarou, and Southern sea monsters. The Letiche is also a cryptid legend found in Louisiana, but it's not as popular as some of the other myths. The story is similar to the legend in this book; the Letiche is an illegitimate, unbaptized child, raised by gators. It lurks in the bayous, upsetting boats, and attacking travelers.

Because of the vagueness surrounding the Letiche legend, the Letiche in *Alligator Skin* is a combination of the original Letiche legend, the Honey Island Swamp Monster, and Rougarou.

What cryptids lurk in your backyard?

ACKNOWLEDGEMENTS

A big thanks to my Lord and Savior, Jesus Christ. Without Him, the things I do would not be possible.

Thank you to my wonderful husband, Kevin. You're amazing at listening to all of my ideas, and talking me through all of my plot holes. I don't know what *Alligator Skin* would have been like without you!

To my family: Thank you for always encouraging my writing! A shout out to my siblings for being the sibling relationship inspiration between Jensen and Linda. Even when we're battling it out, we're still always there for each other in the end, and I'm so grateful for all three of you!

To my beta readers: Thank you for taking the time to sit and read through all the good and bad parts of *Alligator Skin,* and for making the bad parts better.

To Sera: Thank you for your last minute editing skills! I promise to never give you a time crunch like that again.

To R.L. Stine: Thanks for being the best writing inspiration.

To my readers: You guys rock! Thanks for reading. Stay spooky.

ABOUT THE AUTHOR

AudraKate Gonzalez started writing horror stories when she ran out of Goosebumps books to read as a child. Her love for horror grew and now she has a BA in Creative Writing and is working on her MFA. She lives in Ohio with her handsome husband, and her adorable furry bad boys, Zero and Scrappy Doo. When AudraKate isn't writing, you can find her reading, watching scary movies or sleeping. You can follow AudraKate on Instagram or TikTok @lets.get.lit.erature or subscribe to her newsletter by visiting www.authoraudrakategonzalez.com

OTHER BOOKS IN THE
THIS IS NOIR SERIES

Tomato Juice: Something is different about Gran...

It's been years since fourteen-year-old Dean has seen his Gran. After the death of his Paps, the tomato farm he had built started to fail, and Gran sort of just dropped off the face of the earth. But now Dean's mom is desperate to have someone watch him over the summer, which means Dean will be spending his summer with Gran on the farm. He expects his time to be filled with hard work and no Wi-Fi. What ends up happening is a spiral of events that leads him to believe something otherworldly is wrong with Gran. With the help of the pastor's daughter, Felicity, the two will be sent on a mission to find answers about the occult and possession, and discover what lengths someone will go to in order to keep the legacy of a loved one alive.

Made in United States
Cleveland, OH
10 February 2025